A Time To Love

FRANCINE RA'CHELLE

Copyright © 2024 Francine Ra'Chelle

All rights reserved.

ISBN: 9798334863941

No part of this book may be reproduced in any form or by any electronic or mechanical means, including information storage and retrieval systems, without written permission from the author, except in a book review.

Scripture quotations used in this book are from the Holy Bible, New International Version (NIV) and King James Version (KJV).

DEDICATION

I would like to dedicate this book in the loving memories of the two strongest women that I have ever known…

My beautiful, caring and one-of-a-kind mother, Mrs. Ella Francis Dixon Culver. Mama, you were a true soldier throughout your life. I am so thankful and honored to be your daughter and in the twelve years God allowed me to have with you, you taught me life lessons I could use for a lifetime. I love you and miss you every single day. After twenty-two years without you, you still have a great impact on my life. I still have not forgotten you and the awesome woman you were.

My Amazing grandmother, Mrs. Agnes Dixon. Granny, you were the strongest woman and soldier I have ever laid eyes on. You had a heart of gold and I am forever grateful for how you finished raising me after God called Mama home. You taught me so many life lessons. Most importantly, you taught me how to love God and always put him first.

May both of you continue to rest in God's loving arms.

CONTENTS

Chapter One	1
Chapter Two	3
Chapter Three	11
Chapter Four	17
Chapter Five	21
Chapter Six	27
Chapter Seven	29
Chapter Eight	33
Chapter Nine	37
Chapter Ten	39
Chapter Eleven	43
Chapter Twelve	47
Chapter Thirteen	49
Chapter Fourteen	53
Chapter Fifteen	57
Chapter Sixteen	61
Chapter Seventeen	65
Chapter Eighteen	67
Chapter Nineteen	71
Chapter Twenty	73
Chapter Twenty-One	77

Chapter Twenty-Two	79
Chapter Twenty-Three	83
Chapter Twenty-Four	87
Chapter Twenty-Five	89
Chapter Twenty-Six	91
Chapter Twenty-Seven	93
Chapter Twenty-Eight	95
Chapter Twenty-Nine	97
Chapter Thirty	101
Chapter Thirty-One	103
Chapter Thirty-Two	109
Chapter Thirty-Three	111
Chapter Thirty-Four	115
Chapter Thirty-Five	117
Chapter Thirty-Six	121
Chapter Thirty-Seven	125
Chapter Thirty-Eight	129
Chapter Thirty-Nine	133
Chapter Forty	137
Chapter Forty-One	141
Chapter Forty-Two	145
Chapter Forty-Three	149
Chapter Forty-Four	151

A Time to Love

Chapter Forty-Five	153
Chapter Forty-Six	159
Chapter Forty-Seven	163
Chater Forty-Eight	167
Chapter Forty-Nine	173
Epilogue	177
Word from the Author	181
Acknowledgements	183
About the Author	187

Ecclesiastes 3:1&8 KJV

To everything there is a season, and a time to every purpose under the heaven: A time to love, and a time to hate; a time of war, and a time of peace.

~ CHAPTER ONE ~

Biting her bottom lip, Shanti Darwin briefly glanced at the fuchsia clock positioned directly across from her desk on the wall. The white numbers, against the sleek black backdrop of the clock, let her know it was a quarter past five p.m. She had just released her last patient for the day and filled out her remaining charts.

Looking at the pictures on her desk of her, her husband, and their four beautiful children, a smile slowly took over her face as she thought of how blessed she was.

There was something about the entire day that had just seemed a bit different, maybe even a bit off, but she couldn't quite put her fingers on it., She was honestly too drained to even think about it.

As she reached in her desk drawer to retrieve her purse and cell phone, her phone began playing a familiar tune. Monica's hit song, "Why I Love You So Much."

"Hey handsome," she cooed.

"Shanti, we need to talk." Stephon said.

Shanti could feel her heart racing and her throat tightening.

What is going on?

"What's wrong?" she asked once she finally found her voice.

There was a hesitation on the other end.

"Stay where you are. I'm about to come pick you up," he said.

Pushing the desk drawer closed, with trembling hands, she replied. "Stephon tell me what's going on. I mean it."

"I'll tell you when you get in the car," he stated.

Tears formed in her eyes.

There was an uneasy feeling in the pit of her stomach.

What could possibly be going on? Was one of their kids hurt or in danger, was it her parents, grandmother, or his mother? Were all the questions that were racing through her mind.

"Shanti. Are you still there?" he quizzed.

"Ya-ya… yeah," she stammered.

"I'm almost to you. Come outside," he said, ending the call.

Shanti put her phone back inside her purse and began walking to the front entrance. Her heart was pounding like a bass drum through her chest.

"Are you okay Doctor Darwin?" the receptionist Kyra asked. Kyra was a young bubbly girl in her early twenties.

Shanti was too deep in her thoughts to answer her. She walked into the sitting area and plopped down in one of the chairs waiting for Stephon to pull up.

"Doctor Darwin are you okay?" Kyra asked again.

Shanti nodded her head.

A few moments later Stephon drove up in his two-door canary yellow 2023 Camaro. Shanti sashayed to the car at the first glance into his eyes she could tell something was seriously wrong.

~ CHAPTER TWO ~

Shanti took a deep breath before opening the passenger side door and getting in.

"Stephon, I can't take it anymore what's going on?" Shanti asked.

Stephon took his hands off the steering wheel and turned to face her.

In his eyes she could tell he had been crying, fear was streaming from his eyes.

He took her small hands into his, looking heavenward.

"Lord, give me the strength... Shanti there's no easy way to tell you this," he began but paused.

Tears were now welling up in his eyes.

"It's... it's ... your Me-Ma. Her nurse Miss Barbara came in this morning and found her on the kitchen floor unresponsive." Stephon struggled to tell her.

Shanti could feel her throat tightening again.

Tears formed in her own eyes.

How could this happen? This can't be true, I just talked to her before I left for work this morning.

"Are you okay?" Stephon asked.

He leaned over in his seat and pulled her into a hug. The pain from deep down inside her soul erupted causing tears to flow from her eyes like a ruptured volcano.

"Is she still alive?" Shanti asked, once she was able to collect herself.

"Yes, she is, your parents are there waiting on us," Stephon said.

"So, can you give me any details? On what happened to her?" Shanti asked.

"Well like I told you earlier, when Miss Barbara came in this morning to cook her breakfast, she found her on the kitchen floor unresponsive Miss Barbara called 911 and they rushed her to the hospital," Stephon said.

"What hospital is she at Stephon there are three close by?" Shanti asked. "She is at Bale South Medical Center in the Critical Care Unit," Stephon replied.

"What caused her to fall in the kitchen?" Shanti asked.

"Her blood pressure went up too high- she had another stroke. The paramedics said she had one on the way to the hospital. Shanti, Baby from what your mother said when she called me a minute ago the doctors want the whole family there as soon as possible it doesn't look too good," Stephon said, trying to be strong for Shanti.

"I don't know what I'm going to do if she doesn't pull through," she cried out.

Using one hand to prop up her chin so that he could gaze into her eyes, he replied, "Lean on me, I got you Baby."

Shanti brushed his lips with her own. "I know."

"Are you ready to head to the hospital?"

Without uttering a word Shanti nodded her head in agreement.

God, please heal Me-Ma in Jesus name. Shanti prayed to herself. Stephon started the car with one hand on the steering wheel and the other hand gripping Shanti's hand as tightly as he could without hurting her and pulled off.

With Stephon holding her hand tightly they hurried down the hallway and quietly opened the door to the entrance. Shanti's parents were there to greet them. Her mother wiped a single tear from her eyes when she saw Shanti walking towards her.

"Mama, is she okay?" Shanti asked.

Her mother pulled her into a hug. "We don't know yet sweetie."

"Have you called Auntie Mickie?" Shanti asked.

"Yes, I called her four times already, but she didn't answer," Shanti's mother, Lauryn replied.

"That good for nothing boyfriend of her's probably has her phone," Shanti huffed, crossing her arms around her chest and rolling her eyes.

"I hope she calls me back soon."

Lauryn phone began ringing.

"Hello."

"Hey sis. You called?" Mickie asked.

"Yes, Mick I did. Mama isn't doing well I need you to get to the hospital asap," Lauryn said.

"I can't leave right now Jett got to get up for work in a few hours and he needs the car."

Lauryn let's out a deep breath and mumbled something under her breath. "Mickie, this is serious you need to be at this hospital," Lauryn demanded.

There was a moment of silence on the line.

"I'll be there in a few minutes," Mickie said ending the call.

"The Bible says when two are three gather together in His name Jesus is amongst them. Let's join hands and pray to God like never before." Shanti's father, Charles instructed.

Charles, Lauryn, Shanti, and Stephon joined hands and formed a small circle. Charles bowed his head and closed his eyes and everyone else followed.

"Father God Lord Jesus I come to you now humbly as I know how. First, I wanna say thank you for all your many blessing in me and my family's lives and thank you for keeping us safe from harm and danger as we travel to and from work and our homes. Jesus, I pray that you heal the body of My wonderful mother-in-law Ms. Addie Mae Pearson in Jesus name amen."

"Amen," everyone said in unison. Everyone lifted their heads and walked back into the sitting room and sat down waiting for someone to let them know how Me-Ma was doing.

Mickie walked into the sitting area.

Mickie had a butter pecan skin complexion, below the neck length black hair with reddish brown highlights, almond shaped chocolate brown eyes. Her hair was pulled back in a ponytail. She wore a white wrinkled, stained V-neck tee shirt and a pair of loose-fitting black leggings.

What's happened to her? Auntie Mickie used to be so well dressed, kept her hair up. Since she been with Jett, she let herself go.

Mickie walked up to her sister Lauryn, her niece Shanti, Shanti husband Stephon and her brother-in-law Charles and gave each of them a tight hug.

"Hey, Laurie, sorry it took me so long. I got here quick as I could,"

Mickie said.

"It's okay, Mickie," Lauryn replied. "Mickie. What happened to your left eye?" Lauryn asked noticing Mickie's swollen left eye with a red spot covering the right side of the white of her eye.

"I fell in the kitchen," Mickie said.

"That was an ugly fall," Lauryn said reaching out to touch Mickie's face.

"Yeah, it was… how's Mama doing?" Mickie asked changing the subject before Lauryn could ask further questions.

"We don't know, we've been sitting here waiting for over an hour."

A tall muscular built male nurse with a pecan complexion, shaved head and piercing green eyes walked in to greet the family. His navy-blue scrubs compliment his eyes. "Good evening my name is Grant. I am Miss Pearson's nurse for the evening. Miss Pearson just woke up and said that it's urgent she speaks with you all," he said. "You all follow me." He said leading the way down the hallway.

Shanti hurried and opened the door to Me-Ma's room. She covered her mouth and let out a soft cry. The image of seeing her Me-Ma laying in a hospital bed hooked to a ventilator helping her breathe, a heart monitor checking her heart rate and an IV pumping medication into her veins brought tears to her eyes. Shanti collapsed in Stephon's arms. Me-Ma was a full-figured woman, well portioned and thick in all the right places, she had a warm caramel skin tone, shoulder length grey hair that she mostly wore in a low bun at the nape of her neck. Me-Ma had large dark brown round eyes. She had few wrinkles in her face to be an eighty-seven-year-old woman. Her once radiant skin was now dull and pale. Stephon pulled Shanti into his arms and held her tightly as she sobbed.

"Shani girl is that you?" Me-Ma whispered, opening her eyes, and looking over at Shanti.

Shanti wiped the tears from her eyes and sauntered over to her bedside. "Hey Me-Ma."

"I know good and well you're not shedding tears for me," Me-Ma said.

Shanti looked into her eyes and gave her a weak smile.

"Shani Girl, I need something from you," Me-Ma said. There was a pleading in her Me-Ma's eyes that was unmistakable, as though whatever she needed to ask Shanti was the most important thing in her life.

"What is it Me-Ma?"

"I need you to never lose your faith in God," Me-Ma sputtered as she began to cough.

Shanti reached over to grab the water pitcher on the nightstand, but as she went to give Me-Ma a sip of water she shook her head.

"I'm fine child," she said clearing her throat. "Now, as I was saying, I'm getting ready to go home but I need to know you are going to be okay."

Me-Ma I have never been without you. I can't do this.

Instead, Shanti took a deep breath and nodded her head, taking her hand into hers.

"I love you Shani girl."

"I love you more Me-Ma," Shanti whispered.

Me-Ma looked up at Shanti's husband and smiled.

"Boy, you get more handsome every time I see you."

He chuckled softly. "Thank you."

"I want you to promise me something son," Me-Ma said with a more serious look on her face.

"Yes, ma'am anything."

"Promise me… that no matter what life throws at you and Shani Girl you will always find your way back to one another. Allow your love for each other and Jesus be stronger than anything that is thrown at you."

As tears formed in his eyes, he put his arms around Shanti and embraced her. "I promise Me-Ma."

"I believe in you baby. Storms are going to come but your love for God and one another is stronger." Me-Ma said.

"Lauryn, my first born. I want you to continue trusting in God. Be the prayer warrior you always been don't lose your faith. I need you to be strong for the rest of the family and be their strength as I have so many years," Me-Ma said.

"Yes, ma'am I promise."

"Charles, I want you to continue preaching your heart out every Sunday morning and never stop seeking knowledge from God."

"Always," Shanti's father replied, as his voice cracked from him holding back his tears.

"I know yawl ain't in here crying over me. I'm about to go home to be with Lord. I'm ready," Me-Ma said.

"We love you," Shanti's parents said in unison.

"I love yawl too."

Lastly Me-Ma looked over at her youngest daughter and smiled. A single tear rolled down her cheek. "Temetria, I pray that you can one day except Christ into your heart and learn that He is the only answer to all your problems. I hope that you understand these two scriptures one day, Proverbs 3:5-6 learn how to trust in the Lord and allow him to direct your path and Psalm 119:105 the word of Jesus is our light allow him to direct you in the right direction. I love you."

"I will Mama I promise, and I love you too," Mickie whispered, wiping a fresh batch of fallen tears from her eyes.

"I love you all so much."

Beep! Beep!

Grant dashed to Me-Ma's side.

"STAT!" he shouted.

Three other nurses came running.

"We need you all to step out for a moment," one of the nurses ordered, hurrying the family out the room.

Shanti was the last to leave. "I didn't wanna leave her," Shanti sobbed.

Stephon pulled Shanti into his arms she put her arms around his waist and rested her head on his chest and sobbed.

Lauryn turned away from Shanti and Mickie and buried her face into Charles chest sobbing quietly.

Mickie paced the floor back and forth biting her nails something she's always done when she was upset or nervous.

A few moments later Grant walked into the lobby with a blank expression.

"I'm sorry we did everything we could," he said.

"Ahhhhh!" Shanti screamed. Her legs became like noodles she dropped down to her knees. Stephon began cuddling her in his arms.

"It's gonna be okay. I got you Baby," he whispered in her ear.

"Can we see her?" Lauryn asked.

"Yes ma'am. Give us a few moments to clean her up and you can see her," Grant promised. "I am so sorry for your loss." Grant dropped his head and walked through the double doors.

The blinds had been closed and the room was completely dark.

Shanti sauntered into the room clenching on to Stephon's hand sobbing. Her mother and father followed by Mickie walked in behind them. Shanti walked to the left side of the bed and fell to her knees laying her head on Me-Ma's chest.

"Me-Ma, I needed you here with me. I'm not ready to live without you," Shanti cried.

Lauryn walked over to the other side of the bed and fell to Me-Ma's chest hugging her and kissing her cheek, as tears flowed down her face like a waterfall. Mickie sat at her mother's feet. "I love you, Mama," Mickie cried out. Stephon and Charles wrapped their arms around their wives. Stephon gave Mickie a kiss on her cheek and rubbed her back gently.

"We are going to get through this together," Charles said.

~ CHAPTER THREE ~

Temetria "Mickie" Pearson let out a deep sigh before unlocking the door of the three-bedroom house she shared with her boyfriend Jett Beverley.

Stepping onto the threshold she took off her size eight in a half black flip flops and placed them in their resting place on the shoe rack.

"I can't believe my mother's gone. What am I supposed to do?" Mickie busted into tears.

I need Jett to hold me right now.

Mickie walked upstairs heading to their bedroom.

Once she reached the top of the staircase, she could hear a woman's laughter coming from the master bedroom.

"Oh, hell naw! I know this nigga ain't got no female in my bed!" Mickie said, pursing her lips.

Mickie dashed to the door and began pounding with her fist.

"Open this door right now Jett Beverley!"

"Why the hell you beating on the door like the freakin' police?" Jett yelled from the other side.

"I know good and darn well this fool isn't cheatin' on me again! After all that cryin' and beggin' he did last time," Mickie said, clenching her jaw.

Jett swung the door open wearing nothing but a pair of black polka dotted boxer shorts. He was showing off his athletic body. Jett was tall and light skinned, with a low haircut, neatly arched eyebrows, well-trimmed mustache, a soul patch, and a small patch of hair under his chin. He was real eye candy.

"What is yo got damn problem? Why you beatin' on the door like the damn police?" He quizzed, raising his eyebrows, and glaring at Mickie.

"I heard a woman's laugh coming from this room. Who the hell you got in my bed Jett?" She asked, attempting to investigate the room but was stopped when Jett used his body to block her.

"What have I told you about questioning me? You be acting so jealous, and it makes you look foolish! stop doing that."

Tears begin to flow down her cheeks. "Jett, I need you to hold me," Mickie attempted to throw her arms around Jett's shoulders, but he shoved her away from him.

"What are you doing? You know I don't like to be hugged," Jett reminded her.

Mickie lowered her head. "Baby, I need you, my mama passed away earlier."

"Oh, my goodness! Mickie, I'm sorry. I didn't know Me-Ma was sick." Mickie's eyes grew big when she saw her younger cousin Trivia Knowles. Trivia walked to the door wearing nothing but a silk black gown that hugged her perfect figure in all the right places. Trivia was a beautiful woman in an innocent type of way.

"Trivia…what in the fu-," Mickie began but stopped mid-sentence, letting out a deep breath and closing her eyes. "What in the hell you doing here with my man?"

"Mickie wait it's not what you think. Jett and I are just friends," Trivia tried to convince Mickie.

"Hoe you expect me to believe that bull crap! I know you, you're notorious for sleeping around with other women's husbands and boyfriends," Mickie said. She could feel the blood running warm in her veins as her nostrils began to flare up.

Trivia stood back nibbling on her bottom lip and said nothing.

"You know what you think it's a game!" Mickie started taking her diamond earrings out her ears. She charged at Trivia and when she was about to grab her by her arm Jett grabbed Mickie.

"What is your damn problem?" Jett gritted his teeth yelling at Mickie.

"No, what the hell is yo problem bringing this hoe in my house?"

"This is my house; I don't have to explain anything to you!"

"I am your woman, you owe me answers," Mickie shouted.

"I don't owe you shit and if you don't like what I say or how I feel you can get yo shit and get out," he bellowed.

Before Mickie could say another word, Jett stormed to the dresser drawers that contained her clothing and begin throwing them on the floor.

"You think I'm playing with you Mickie? Get out of my house!" He yelled even louder than before causing her and Trivia to jump.

"Jett, please… I don't have anywhere to go," Mickie cried once she finally found her voice.

"I don't care… get out now!"

"Please don't do this… I have no place to go," she begged, as tears begin rolling down her cheeks. "You can bring whoever you want in here please don't kick me out!"

"I don't care get out and by the way give me my phone back," he said snatching her cellphone out her 38C cup bra.

"Jett please don't put me out. I'm sorry I'll never question you again."

"Mickie get out of my face before I end up hurting you," he replied.

"Jett no, please!"

Jett shoved Mickie so hard she hit the floor. He grabbed her by her arms and dragged her downstairs.

"Jett please stop!" She cried, kicking, and screaming.

Trivia stood dumbfounded and watched as he dragged Mickie out the door. Mickie was kicking and screaming begging him to stop. He slammed the door shut and ran back upstairs to get her belongings.

Mickie pounded on the door begging him to let her back in. He opened the door long enough to throw her belongings into the yard.

Sobbing, Mickie stood and began picking up her clothes scattered around the yard.

Mickie wiped at her fallen tears. "I don't know what I'm going to do but I'm going to be okay."

She looked back at the front door hoping Jett would have mercy on her and let her back into their home. Once she realized that was not going to happen she grabbed the little clothes she could carry in her arms and began walking up the street barefoot sobbing to herself.

"My mama just passed away my man is cheating on me with my blood relative and kicked me out for it. What a day?" Mickie chuckled through her tears. Mickie walked two blocks to the nearest gas station the Hobo Pantry. Her feet were throbbing and sore, but she knew she had to make it to the store. Mickie walked inside the store and towards the front counter sweat was dripping down her face, she could barely catch her breath. The store manager was standing behind the counter wiping down and humming to himself. Mr. Bob had been a friend of the family since Mickie was a small child. He used to work at a production plant named Kleinert with her father until her father retired. Mr. Bob was tall, heavy set built, with a dark chocolate skin tone, and a shaved head.

"Hey Mickie. What can I do for you?" He asked in a deep baritone voice.

"May I use your phone?" Mickie asked, once she could finally speak.

"Sure," he replied, reaching one hand under the counter. "Is everything okay? You look like you have a lot going on right now."

"My mom just passed away," Mickie whispered, still trying to process the news.

"Oh, my goodness, I am so sorry. Mickie I didn't even know my Addie was sick," Mr. Bobby said.

"She had a stroke," Mickie said.

Mr. Bobby handed Mickie his iPhone 15 Pro max.

Mickie dialed her best friend Azure Kelly's number and put the phone to her ear.

"Hello," Azure answered.

"Hey Azure. It's Mickie can you please come pick me up from Mr. Bobby's store?" Mickie asked.

"What's going on?" Azure queried.

"Jett put me out again and to top it off my mama just died," Mickie blurted out.

"Girl I'm on my way," Azure said ending the call.

Azure drove up in her midnight blue 2016 Nissan Maxima with chrome wheels and tinted windows. Azure was a natural beauty, she had long black Afro kinky hair, butter pecan skin, large chestnut brown round eyes.

"What's wrong boo?" Azure asked soon as Mickie sat down in the passenger seat and throw her clothes in the back.

"Well, you know my mom just passed away. I came back from the hospital to find Jett laid up with Trivia," Mickie informed her friend.

Azure opened her mouth wide and raised her neatly arched eyebrows. "Girl! Are you freakin' serious?" Azure asked.

"Yes I am."

"I really had high hopes for that girl. I thought she would have turned out differently, especially since she watched her mother suffer and die from an STD," Azure replied.

"True... but I guess she doesn't care or Jett," Mickie said.

"I know you are not going back to him after this. Mickie that is low down and dirty screwing yo blood like that. And how could she even do that to you when your mother took her nasty behind in after her mother died," Azure stated.

"I don't know," Mickie said.

"Mickie you know I got your back," Azure said.

"I know," Mickie said softly.

"I am gonna help you through this," Azure assured Mickie holding her hand.

"Thank you Azure that means a lot," Mickie replied with a smile.

~ CHAPTER FOUR ~

It was the morning of the funeral Shanti was feeling awful. She sat in the guest room holding her Me-Ma's favorite gray sweater in her arms. It still smelled like her.

"Me-Ma I can't believe you are gone forty-two years was not enough time with you." Shanti sobbed, inhaling the perfume.

Shanti's mind drifted back to when she was seven. A small girl full of energy. On this particular day she was wearing a white T-SHIRT and pale pink overalls, her long silky black hair was in two pigtails with the matching pink ponytail holders.

"Shanti, do you wanna go to Memphis for the three-night tent revival with me and your father or do you wanna stay with Mama for a few days?" Lauryn asked, walking into Shanti's room.

Shanti was sitting on her bed watching Looney Tunes and brushing her Barbie doll's hair.

"I'll stay with Me-Ma," Shanti replied.

"Come in the living room and call her to see if she's busy," Lauryn suggested.

Shanti jumped off her full-sized bed with the Mario Brothers bed set and ran down the hall into the living room. Shanti picked up the receiver and dialed Me-Ma's number, using the touch tone phone.

"Good morning, the Pearson residence," Me-Ma answered.

"Hey Me-Ma, it's me Shanti."

"Hey there, Shani Girl!" Me-Ma replied, sounding chipper to hear from her granddaughter.

"Can I come spend a few days with you while my parents go to

Memphis for revival?" Shanti asked.

"Of course, you can. I'm going to the pea field early tomorrow morning," Me-Ma said.

"That's fine I like picking peas with you," Shanti said honestly.

Shanti reminisced running up the driveway to Me-Ma's dark brown brick three-bedroom bungalow. Her long black hair was typed in a bun, and she wore a white button-down house dress with purple flowers and a pair of soft purple house slippers, smelling like Candid Avon perfume.

"I made a fresh batch of chocolate chip cookies. Do you wanna eat a few cookies, drank us a tall glass of milk and play Barbie dolls?" Me-Ma asked.

"Yes ma'am."

"Hey Mama, are you okay?" Shanti's fourteen-year-old daughter Harmony asked. Harmony was a beautiful girl. She was about five feet and two inches tall, with silky shoulder length black hair, nicely arched eyebrows, naturally long black eyelashes, and chocolate brown oval shaped eyes.

"Yes, Princess I'm okay."

Harmony walked to Shanti and threw her arms around her neck. "I love you Mama and we are all going to get through this together."

"I know," Shanti replied wiping away a fresh batch of tears that had formed in her eyes.

"Grandma and Papa are in the living room," Harmony said.

Clearing her throat. The realization that her grandmother's funeral was happening soon settled inside her heart causing a sudden onslaught of loneliness and sadness.

"Okay, tell them I'll be there in a few minutes."

"Okay," Harmony said excusing herself.

Dear Lord. Give me the strength to do this I can't do this by myself. *I am close to the broken hearted and I save those who are crushed in spirit.*

The voice sounded so real that Shanti looked around to be sure she was alone.

She took a deep breath before standing to her feet and walking into the living room.

Her parents sat on the loveseat decked out in their matching attire.

Lauryn was a beautiful, strong woman. She has an espresso skin tone, thin eyebrows and short natural eyelashes, dark brown round shaped eyes, glossy wide lips, and a button nose. Lauryn looked gorgeous in her two-piece houndstooth pattern knee-length dress suit with a short sleeve black jacket, a black crown covering her head and a pair of open toe black sandal heels. The dress hugged her small frame in all the right places.

Charles was wearing a solid black shawl collar front button blazer and pants suit with a white-collar shirt and black button-down vest and black loafers. Charles has a hot cocoa skin complexion, tall, buff built with a pot belly, a button nose, wide-set eyes, and a clean smooth head.

When Lauryn saw her daughter, she stood to her feet to greet her.

"Hey baby, how are you holding up?" She asked still embracing her.

"I'm okay Mama. I miss her already."

"I know baby so do I."

"Hey there baby girl," her father said taking her into his arms.

She rested her head on his chest.

"Hey Daddy," she said.

"How are you feeling?" he asked.

"I'm okay," she said.

"I know it's hard, but we are all going to get through this together," he said putting his arms around both Shanti and her mother.

A few minutes later the men entered the living room. Shanti couldn't take her eyes off Stephon. He stood tall at six foot three inches with a peanut butter complexion, almond-shaped chocolate brown eyes, low-cut hair with deep waves, well maintained beard, and mustache. When he made eye contact with Shanti, he displayed a smile as big as a crescent moon, revealing two deep dimples in his cheeks. He looked amazing decked out in his white with black trims down the front step collar, one button two-piece pants suit, their oldest two sons Sha'Bron "Bron" and Xavion matched him. They towered over their mother. One by one they walked over to her and gave her a hug before going to greet their grandparents.

Shanti sauntered over to Stephon. She angled her head so that her eyes were able to travel the length of him. "Wow Mr. Darwin you look amazing."

"Thank you, Mrs. Darwin, so do you," he said, admiring the tea length dress she wore.

He pulled her into his arms and held her. "I love you my black queen and I got you always."

"I know Stephon. I love you too." She held on to their embrace for a few seconds more knowing it was the safest place for her in a time like this. She didn't let go until their friends Rasheia and her husband Rashad, Casmira, Yasmine, and her husband Brandon walked over to offer their condolences.

"Hey how are you guys doing?" Rasheia asked pulling Shanti into a hug and then Stephon. The navy-blue button-down blouse complimented her radiant hazelnut skin complexion and her small dark brown eyes. Rasheia has a button nose and glossy thin lips.

"I'm good. Thank you for coming," Shanti replied.

"You are more than welcome. If you need anything let me and Shad know," Rasheia said.

"I will thank you so much Sheia," Shanti said.

Her husband Rashad then gave Shanti a hug and afterwards gave Stephon a brotherly hug.

"I'm praying for you all," Rashad said.

"Thank you," Shanti and Stephon said in unison.

"Awe, Shani, I love you girl Casmira replied hugging Shanti.

"I love you too," Shanti said.

"We are all praying for you and your family," Yasmine said.

"Oh yeah Shanti I forgot to tell you Audria and Gabe, and Talia and Jacob are all running behind. They said they would meet us at the church and to let you know they love you and they're sorry for your loss," Rasheia said.

"Okay thank you for letting me know," Shanti said.

"We are all here if you need us," Brandon chimed in.

"Thank you, guys." Stephon and Shanti said in unison.

After their friends shared their condolences, the funeral directors came. Shanti held Stephon's hand as tight as she could.

~ CHAPTER FIVE ~

Stephon Darwin held Shanti's hand as tightly as he possibly could without hurting her. Out the corners of his eyes he could see her sobbing as they made their way inside the church

"Let not your heart be troubled ye believe in God, believe also in me.

In my Father's house are many mansions if it were not so, I would have told you. I go to prepare a place for you.

And if I go and prepare a place for you, I will come again, and receive you unto myself; that where I am, there ye may be also," Pastor Cox, a family friend read while they walked in.

Ms. Addie Mae Pearson better known to him as Me-Ma looked so peaceful in her white dress and matching white headband with a white rose on the left side that she wore every Sunday morning with her white pearls around her neck.

He watched intensely as his wife bent down and gave her a kiss on her cheek.

"She looks so at peace," Shanti whispered to him.

"Yes, she does, and I believe she is," he said back, walking her to their seat on the second row. After they were seated, he watched as their four children marched beside one another. The boys lead their two younger sisters like the gentlemen they were raised to be. It made him proud that his sons were becoming the leaders he so desperately wanted them to be.

Once everyone was seated, the choir sang two selections before Pastor Cox walked to the pulpit.

"If anyone would like to share memories of Mother Addie Mae Pearson you may speak now but only for a maximum of five minutes, please." He said before taking his seat again.

A petite lady with shoulder length black hair sashayed up to the front of the church. "Good afternoon, everyone my name is Elena Fryer. I have known Ms. Addie better known as Me-Ma for over ten years now. When my ex-husband left me, I was broken and alone until the day I met Me-Ma. She walked up to me in the supermarket and asked me was I okay. I lied and told her yes; to make a long story short, I told her about my troubles. She bought my groceries that day and until a few weeks ago she made sure my three children and I had everything we needed, and she introduced me to Christ. I am forever grateful for her." The young lady said taking a Kleenex and wiping her eyes.

The young lady took her seat, and a gentleman approached after her.

Stephon looked over at Shanti and realized she was sobbing so hard she was shaking. To get her through the remainder of the service he placed his arms around her and gently kissed her cheek as she settled in his arms.

"Evening everyone. I wouldn't be standing before you all today if it weren't for Me-Ma. You see, I was homeless. I'd lost my job. Day after day people shunned me and looked down upon me. One day Me-Ma walked past, and she stopped. Child you ain't nothing but skin and bones when's the last time you ate something.

It's been a while I told her.

She didn't change any words she walked inside McDonald's and grabbed me a meal. After that she told me come with me young man and took me to her house not knowing me at all and allowed me to stay in her guest room. I stayed with her doing odd chores until I got on my feet, and she never allowed me to pay her back. She said me turning my life around and excepting Christ Jesus into my life was payback enough. To know her was to love her and I am forever grateful," he said wiping tears from his eyes.

After everyone who wished to speak shared their memories. Pastor Cox took the pulpit again.

"Mother Addie Mae Pearson better known to us all as Me-Ma was a strong and compassionate woman. I am so glad I got the opportunity to know her and be a part of her family for over forty plus years. I remember the first time I ever met her I was still in the world. After attending a party with a couple friends one of the guys thought it would be a joke to lace the weed. I nearly died that night, but I made it to Me-Ma's house she prayed over me and never told my parents. I am saved today because of her," he said.

The congregation begin to clap their hands.

Me-Ma was one incredible woman. Stephon thought back to when he first met Me-Ma. She was sitting in her living room wearing a black button-down house coat with the matching turban wrap on her head. She was leaned back in her grey recliner watching an episode of In the Heat of the Night, shelling a bowl of peas.

He was nervous about meeting her because first meeting with her parents didn't go so well.

"Hey Me-Ma, this is Stephon and Stephon this my Me-Ma," Shanti introduced them.

"Hey Stephon, how are you?" Me-Ma asked.

"I'm fine," he said nervously.

"I hear that you are seeing my baby. Are you treating her right?" Me-Ma asked.

"Yes ma'am, Stephon said, nodding his head in agreement.

"Well, that's all that matters as long as my Shani Girl is happy I'm happy," Me-Ma said with a pleasant smile.

She loved him and treated him like he was her own grandson. Me-Ma was the only grandmother he knew. Their love for one another and bond lasted a lifetime. Another memory materialized in his mind. He and Shanti had their first disagreement as a married couple. Shanti ran up Me-Ma's steps carrying their son Sha'Bron in her arms. Shanti opened the wooden screen door and slammed it hard.

"Gal, what's wrong wit you slamming my door like you ain't got no sense?" Me-Ma chastised her.

"I'm sorry Me-Ma but Stephon made me so angry," Shanti said.

Stephon stood back in the doorway just in case he needed to make a run for it.

"Hand me this baby," Me-Ma said, reaching out and taking Sha'Bron from Shanti and laying him down in the playpen. "Both of yawl go in the kitchen and wait on me."

"Now what seems to be the problem?" Me-Ma asked, looking at both Stephon and Shanti.

"Me-Ma, Stephon doesn't help me around the house or with the baby like he should," Shanti stated her case.

"Okay I see let me hear your side Stephon," Me-Ma said.

"I don't have any excuses Me-Ma. It's like this once I get off work I be tired. I take a shower and lay down. I don't think about the day Shanti's had," Stephon said.

"How about this… the two of you sit down and communicate with one another come up with a solution that involves the two of you taking turns and taking some slack off the other one," Me-Ma suggested.

"I like that idea," Stephon and Shanti said in unison.

"See marriage is all about communication," Me-Ma said.

When his mind came back to the present. Pastor Cox was still talking.

"I know for a fact Mother Addie Mae is in heaven rejoicing with the Lord. When I think of her a song comes to mind."

"Glory Glory Hallelujah since I laid my burdens down.

Glory Glory Hallelujah since I laid my burdens down. Every round goes higher and higher since I laid my burdens down. Church I'm going home to live with Jesus since I laid my burdens down. I'm going home to live with Jesus since I laid my burdens down."

When he finished singing there wasn't a dry eye in the church.

After the service, the repast was held inside Shanti and Stephon's 120 sq ft vinyl rectangular eight wall gazebo with the evergreen roof located in the backyard behind their emerald, green lake. As a final tribute to the Mother of the church the Mothers board did not attend the funeral they stayed at the house and made sure the gazebo and food was sat up and prepared properly.

Shanti knew the feeling she was feeling wasn't right but for some reason she wanted to blame herself for her Me-Ma's death.

If I hadn't been too busy trying to chase a degree. I could have been with her and not have a total stranger taking care of her. I put my own needs before her needs.

"Baby are you okay? You haven't said a word since we got back." Stephon asked.

"Yes, I'm fine, just thinking about Me-Ma," she said.

"She's in a better place now," he said.

"That's what everyone keeps telling me, but I miss her so much," she said dapping at her eyes with a Kleenex she had in her hand.

"I know you do, hold on to all the memories you shared over the years," he replied.

Nodding her head, she excused herself walked to the lake. Taking a lawn chair and plopping down, tears instantly escaped from her eyes.

A few moments later her mother joined her.

"Are you okay?" Lauryn asked as soon as she saw her daughter.

Wiping the tears from her eyes, Shanti nodded her head in affirmation.

"Awe... baby I know you are hurting, and you miss her. I do too."

"Mama. I can't help but feel it's my fault. If I wasn't too busy chasing degrees and money. She wouldn't have been alone," she sobbed.

"Baby girl it wasn't your fault. You have a family who needs you. Mama didn't want you worrying about her," Mama replied.

"I know, but I'm left with all these unanswered questions and feelings," Shanti said.

"I know baby, but we still got to push through; we promised her."

"I know. It's easier said than done," Shanti replied.

Lauryn pulled her daughter into her arms and embraced her. "It is going to be okay. We are going to get through this somehow."

Shanti wrapped her arms around her mother's waist and cried.

~ CHAPTER SIX ~

Old school music was blasting from the speakers, laughter and loud chattering came from every direction. The aroma of soul food filled the air.

Mickie sat alone at a round table watching while everyone else interact. The feeling of loneliness came over her, how was it she was in a relationship with the man she loved but still felt like an outcast. Life hasn't always been fair to her leaving a void in her heart and soul, she longed for something, but she didn't know what it was.

Azure sashayed over to Mickie's table and sat down beside her.

"Hey boo, how's it going?" Azure asked pulling Mickie into a tight hug.

"I feel lost, broken and alone," Mickie replied.

"Jesus Christ is close to the brokenhearted. I know you don't wanna hear this, but he is the only one that can heal your heart and give you peace, comfort and understanding," Azure said.

"I know Azure, but I'm too messed up right now," Mickie said.

"Mickie, you are never to messed up for Jesus to help you and heal you. Come to church with me sometime and I promise you will feel better," Azure assured Mickie.

Azure gave Mickie another hug and kiss on the cheek.

"I love you girl," Azure said.

"I love you too," Mickie said.

Azure excused herself from the table.

Mickie glanced over in the corner and seen Jett hugging and whispering something in Trivia's ear. Whatever he said must have been funny both were laughing hysterically and touching on one another. Apart of her wanted to march over there and snatch him away from her but she knew the outcome would be something for which she wasn't ready.

Trivia eyeballed her as she leaned in closer to Jett.

Something in her gut was telling her Jett was not the man she thought he was, even though when rough times came, he would have her back because having a piece of man was better than having nothing at all right? And he was at least trying to make her happy.

"Mickie, I know you don't want to hear this, but you need to learn to put yourself first," Lauryn said. Taking a chair and sitting next to her.

"What are you talking about Laurie?"

"Mickie, Jett is over there socializing with other people when he should be here comforting you," Lauryn replied.

First, I hear it from my mother and friends now I hear it from my own sister. I'm so tired of people trying to tell me how to feel Jett is a good man in his own way.

"Mickie, are you okay?" Lauryn quizzed.

No, I'm not okay, I just buried my mother, and my sister is on my back.

"Yes, Laurie, I'm okay."

"Mickie, it's okay to hurt and it's okay to express your feelings."

I am not in the mood for one of Laurie's long lectures right now. "I'm going to get me something to drink," Mickie said, before excusing herself from the table.

~ CHAPTER SEVEN ~

As he ran his left hand slowly up and down her right thigh. Jett Beverley give a seductive look in Trivia's direction when she made eye contact with him.

First, she jerked her leg away and shake her head in disagreement.

"What's wrong with you?" he asked leaning closer and whispering in her ear.

"Jett this is wrong, you don't think so?" she asked.

"Neither one of us are married," he responded.

"I can't help but feel I'm doing Mickie wrong."

"How would you be doing her wrong first? And secondly why are you worried about her?"

"I have a conscience," she replied.

"Do you see a ring on my finger?" he asked moving his hand side to side.

"No," she whispered barely loud enough for him to hear.

"Okay then we are not doing anything wrong. Like I told you a second ago I'm not married to Mickie and to be honest I don't plan on ever tying the knot with her."

"Jett, she is my cousin. I don't want to hurt her," she replied.

"How are you going to hurt her? Mickie knows what's really going on. I've been telling her for months now. Don't wanna be with her anymore."

Jett leaned in closer and kissed Trivia's cheek. "I don't want Mickie, I want you."

A tear slowly rolled down Trivia's cheek.

"I wanna be with you too."

Jett began to think about the past eight years. He'd met Mickie through one of his homeboys. She was young, full of life and beautiful back then. She was thick in all the right places; her body was fit but after so long she begins to let herself go. Now she was bigger, the finest was long gone and she didn't bother to fix herself up anymore. Trivia on the other hand was slender, built with nice curves she was every man's dream.

"Jett are you okay?" Trivia asked.

"Yeah, I'm fine, are you ready to get out of here and go have some one-on-one time?" he asked.

"What about?" Was all she managed to get out before he gave a mean look.

Trivia knew what that look meant, she stood up from her seat to say her goodbyes to her family.

What man in his right mind wants to be with a woman who can't follow simple directions? He thought to himself as he Reminisce on his relationship with Mickie.

It was hardly a day that went by they didn't argue about her not cleaning the house or cooking. He was the bread winner all he asked was for her to cook, clean and pay the bills she couldn't even do that right and when he brought it to her attention, she always had an excuse as to why she didn't do as she was told. After eight years of trying to make their relationship work, he was over it. He wanted someone who would appreciate him and love him the way he wanted to be loved.

Trivia was that person. She listened to him and did everything he told her to do without him having to raise his voice or get mean with her.

"I'm ready," she said.

"Okay, let's get out of here."

As they reached the front door, he saw Mickie walking back inside.

"Where are you two going?" she asked blocking the doorway looking from him to her for answers.

Rolling his eyes. "Mickie, what have I told you about asking me where I'm going? I'm a grown man and unlike you, I pay my own bills and don't depend on anybody else to do it for me," Jett retorted.

"Jett, I don't care about that bull crap you talkin.' You should still give me a little bit of respect. I just buried my mother for heaven's sake," Mickie replied.

"Mickie get out of my way before I embarrass you," he said gritting his teeth. "Think about where you lay your head every night and who provides that."

Mickie dropped her head and moved aside.

It made Jett feel good that Mickie was so submissive to him.

A smile spread across his face as he walked to his car with Trivia on his arm.

~ CHAPTER EIGHT ~

Surrounded by the hot water and steam of the shower, Trivia Knowles reflects on the intimate encounter she shared with her boyfriend Jett.

Jett Beverley made her forget everything and everybody in the last past hour. It felt good to forget and escape the world around her even if it was only for a moment.

As the water ran down her body Trivia thought back to when she was a young teenager, her mother was not like most mothers teaching their daughters how to work and maintain a stable life for themselves. She taught her to use her good looks and body to get everything she wanted and needed from a man, by the time Trivia turned twelve she had curves that super models wished for.

It was one early morning before school Trivia remembered vividly. Her mother Nikole was still lying in bed with an empty whiskey bottle on the floor beside her and a half-smoked cigarette and joint resting in the ash tray. Trivia walked over to her side of the bed and shook her to wake her up.

"What do you want girl? I'm trying to sleep," her mother growled at her.

"Mama, I don't like the way the old men look at me when I walk to the bus stop," Trivia recalled telling her mother that summer morning.

"You have a cute shape that's nothing to be ashamed of," her mother told her.

"I just don't like being stared at like I'm a piece of filet mignon," Trivia whined.

"Nonsense you have a gift why don't you work it," her mother said.

"What do you mean?" Trivia inquired.

"You have nice hips, thighs, and butt something a lot of women are lacking and what every man desires in a woman use it to your advantage to make men throw themselves at your feet. Look at your Mama I don't want for nothing. Why? Because I know how to flaunt my body," her mother told her.

"I don't wanna be like that Mama. I want to be independent," Trivia whined.

"That's nonsense why work your fingers to the bone when you can have a man give you everything you desire?" her mother informed her.

"Mama, I don't want to be that kind of girl," Trivia said.

Trivia's mother grabbed her by her pink shirt pulling her close to her until she was eye level with her. Trivia was so close to her mother she could feel her breath in her face.

"Little girl let me tell you something I have taken care of you all your miserable little life you will not turn your nose up at me and think you are above me. I am proud of who I am and what I do. I ain't soft, burned out and weak like the rest of these women," her mother snared.

Trivia swallowed hard before nodding her head in confirmation.

"You see this man lying next to me right now," her mother began and paused to rise the cover so Trivia could see the gentleman in bed with her.

"Yes ma'am," Trivia whispered.

"He's married but he makes sure I have everything I want and need now that's what I'm talking about don't settle for an everyday nine to five girl with a body like that."

Another thought came to her mind.

Trivia never questioned anything her mother told her because she thought her mother was always right and would never steer her in the wrong direction.

That was until one afternoon when Trivia was fourteen years old, she came home from school like any other day and threw her backpack on the floor by the door and walked into the living room, her mother was sitting on the couch with her male friend Dennis hugged up. "Hey pumpkin, how was school" her mother asked.

"It was okay," Trivia shrugged her shoulders trying to make small talk so she could run down the hall to her room. There was something about Dennis that did not sit well with Trivia, and she could not put her fingers on it.

"Why are you trying to hurry off to your room come speak to Dennis," her mother instructed her.

"Mama, I have a project I need to finish by tomorrow," Trivia lied.

"Girl, you have plenty of time, come in here for a minute," her mother said.

Trivia sashayed into the living room. She could tell both her mother and Dennis were drunk and high off only they knew what. Trivia's heart was beating like a bass drum when she sat on the opposite couch of her mother and Dennis and without fell Dennis began eyeballing her like she was a piece of candy making her feel uneasy and uncomfortable.

Why do my Mama keep making me come around this man? I know she sees how he looks at me and it's *disgusting and rude.* Trivia remembered thinking to herself.

"Hey Trivia, how was school today?" he asked looking down at her fully developed bosom and licking his lips.

"It was fine," Trivia replied barely above a whisper. Trivia tried to cover her chest with her hands.

"Trivia, sweetheart, Dennis and I were just talking I need a couple extra dollars on the electric bill can you help me out?" her mother asked.

"What can I do?" Trivia asked.

"You remember that talk we had about you have a nice body?" her mother began and stop making sure Trivia understood her and was following along.

"Yes ma'am."

"Dennis wants you to undress for him don't worry he's not going to hurt you I'll be right here the whole time," her mother said.

"No! I'm not going to do that!" Trivia shrieked.

"All these years I've taken care of you, and when I need you, you can't help me?" her mother yelled at her.

"Mama, I don't wanna show that man my body," Trivia cried out loud.

"I don't see any harm in it, I did it for my mother to help pay bills," her mother informed her.

Trivia remembered walking down the hall to her room with her mother and Dennis in tow walking over to her bed and sitting down.

"Stand up and take your clothes off very slow," Dennis demanded her.

"Mama!" Trivia cried but her mother stood back in the corner and said nothing.

"Hey Trivia, are you okay in there?" Jett yelled from her bedroom interrupting her thoughts.

"Yes, I'm fine," Trivia said wiping a fresh batch of tears from her eyes.

Mama why did you do that to me? Now I feel like my body is all every man cares about.

Trivia stepped out the shower and wrapped her towel around her before walking to the mirror to blow dry her hair. When she looked up Jett was standing there staring at her.

"Wow you are so beautiful," he said.

"Thank you," Trivia purred.

Jett walked over to her and put his arms around her waist. "I love you and only Trivia."

As much as she wanted to believe him, she couldn't her heart and trust in people especially men had been broken a long time ago.

~ CHAPTER NINE ~

The sound of her heels clicking from the pair of shoes she wore making their way down what seemed like a never-ending corridor.
Finally, she and the prison guard made their way to the end of the hallway.

"Right this way ma'am," the female guard said opening the door and leading her into a small dark room.

Lauryn Laughlin sat down in the hard, cold, metal chair, placing her purse on the table in front of her.

How had things gotten so bad for her only sister that she was driven to commit a crime?

After what seemed like a century the guard was finally back with Mickie, the image of seeing her in handcuffs and shackles on her feet brought tears to Lauryn's eyes. She wanted so desperately to run over to her and take off the cuffs and shackles. Mickie looked so pitiful like she had lost her best friend in the whole world. Lauryn watched intensely while the guard unchained her and excused herself to give them privacy.

Instantly Mickie threw her body into Lauryn's embrace.

"Oh, my goodness, what happened Mickie?"

"I don't know Laurie. I just lost it when I came home and found Jett with another woman," Mickie said wiping the fresh fallen tears from her eyes.

"Mickie, I don't know what to say. I am so sorry this happened to you, you didn't deserve this," Lauryn replied.

"How much time are they trying to give me?" Mickie asked.

The lawyer's voice saying life without parole for two accounts of first-degree murder came to Lauryn's mind.

"You don't need to be thinking about that right now, you not to be thinking about getting yourself together and your head on right," Lauryn replied.

"I'm so sorry I let you and everybody else down, especially Mama," Mickie sobbed.

Lauryn pulled Mickie into her arms and hugged her as tightly as she possibly could. The scene shifted to a hospital room Lauryn was walking slowly to a hospital bed. The doctor and nurses were working hard to save them, but it seemed as though all hope was gone.

"We lost her," the doctor said.

When Lauryn finally looked down to see who was laying there.

"Oh my gosh no!" She started screaming.

"Laurie, Baby wake up," her husband Charles replied wrapping his arms around her.

Lauryn looked up and saw her husband.

"Oh my gosh! Charles that dream was horrible," Lauryn cried. She threw her arms around his neck and sobbed on his shoulder.

"Tell me about it," Charles said.

"First, I dreamed Mickie was in jail for two accounts of murder and then I dreamed..." Lauryn began and paused putting her hands over her mouth as tears spilled down her cheeks. "Take your time, Baby," Charles whispered, massaging her neck.

"Charles. I dreamed our baby girl died," Lauryn blurted out, starting to cry again.

"Oh my…my…my… Jesus. What can possibly go on with Shanti? Let us pray for her and Mickie and then I'm calling my baby girl to check on her," Charles replied.

Lauryn nodded her head in agreement, still shaken by her dream. She and Charles got out of bed and began praying.

~ CHAPTER TEN ~

Shanti sat quietly at her desk looking over patients' charts trying to catch up from being out for almost two weeks.
The conversation she had with her husband before she left was still fresh on her mind.

"Baby, are you sure you're up to going back to work?" He asked.

Letting out a long sigh she replied. "These bills are not going to pay themselves, are they?"

I didn't hesitate to go in to work when Me-Ma needed me why should I hesitate to now. There I go doing it again blaming myself.

"If you need more time, I can cover the expenses, you don't look completely ready," he said. "Is something worrying you?"

"No Stephon I'm fine," she snapped.

Shaking his head and raising his hands in defeat he walked away.

The last couple days she's found herself getting smart with him and their children whenever they said something to her. She didn't know exactly what was happening to her.

With the blinking of her eyes, the thoughts were gone, and she was staring at the charts in front of her.

"Good morning, Doctor Darwin," her best friend and physician assistant Casmira greeted Shanti with a smile entering her office. Casmira and Shanti has been friends since Pre-K. Casmira was a beautiful woman and single mother of four, she has a light honey skin complexion, heart shaped lips, deep set dark brown eyes, a button nose and thick, long, and silky wavy black hair. She is black mixed with Puerto Rican.

"Morning Cassie," she replied.

Casmira walked over to her desk and placed a cup of Starbucks coffee and breakfast on her desk. "I thought you needed this pick me up on your first day back."

"Awe thanks, Cassie," Shanti said, standing from her chair and pulling Casmira into a much-needed hug.

"I love you girlie, and you know I got your back."

"I know Cassie and thank you."

"How are you doing? Are you okay?" Casmira asked.

"I'm okay, I guess. I miss her like crazy."

"I can only imagine you were with her all the time. Do you remember that time when she was babysitting all of us and we dared Yasmine to go into the woods behind her house and she got lost for over three hours?"

"Yes, and when Me-Ma found her we all got our behinds beat," Shanti said.

"Those were the good old days," Casmira replied.

"Yes, they were."

"I'm going to let you get back to work I'm across the hall if you need me," Casmira said.

"Thank you."

Me-Ma was one of a kind. Me-Ma was there more times than her own parents had been. That was why Shanti could not help but think, she had let her Me-Ma down.

Shanti continued to rattle through her paperwork and make notes of upcoming appointments.

She begins looking through one of her elderly patient's charts, the lady was a close friend and next-door neighbor of Me-Ma's sadness entered her heart uncontrollable tears begin to flow down her face.

"Why my Me-Ma? Why?" She cried out. As tears ruptured from her eyes. Her shoulders slumped over, and her body begin to shake uncontrollably as the tears flowed down like a waterfall.

Casmira heard her cries and went into her office from across the hall. "Shanti, are you sure, okay?"

"I want answers Cassie, of all people why my grandmother," she cried.

"Shanti you are going to get through this I promise you."

"Why did God have to take her? I needed her here with me," Shanti cried, hitting the top of her desk.

"Shanti, do you need to go home and get yourself together," Casmira asked, wiping the tears from Shanti's eyes.

Although she tried to speak the words would not come out, Casmira grabbed her briefcase from the back of her chair and through it around her neck, reaching into her desk drawer she grabbed her purse after she made sure she had all of Shanti's important items she helped her up from her seat and walked her out the side door making sure no one seen her in her vulnerable stage.

Stephon was standing in the driveway pacing back and forth impatiently waiting for Casmira's black Honda accord to pull up. Casmira had called him on his way out the door to tell him she was bringing Shanti home. She had a severe crying episode that morning and he could hear her crying while Casmira was talking to him.

"Father God Lord Jesus, please heal Shanti's broken heart and make her whole," he prayed aloud. It hurt so bad that he couldn't take away her hurt and pain, but he knew that nothing was impossible for Christ Jesus.

A few moments later Casmira pulled into the driveway, he rushed over to the passenger side, swinging open the door. Seeing his wife in so much pain and grief almost brought tears to his own eyes. As he lifted her body into his arms and carried her into their home Casmira followed behind him carrying her belongings and shoes.

"Do you need me to stay here with her?" Casmira asked.

"No, I'll work from home for a while to make sure she's fine," Stephon said.

"You got my number Sty, don't hesitate to use it," Casmira said.

"Thanks Cassie. Please continue to pray for her," Stephon said.

"Always, love you guys."

"Love you too."

Casmira gave Stephon a hug before getting in her car and disappearing down the street.

"Come on baby let me take you upstairs," he replied. Lifting Shanti into his arms once more.

Once she was safely in bed, he laid down behind her. "it's going to be okay."

"No, it's not Sty, my grandmother is gone and she's not coming back. I want to curl up and die," Shanti cried.

"Don't say that baby, you have so much to live for."

"Yeah, like what?"

"You have your job; those patients need you. Your kids need their mother, your parents need you and last but not least I need my wife, my best friend and good fine thang."

A light chuckle escaped from her mouth.

"You are so goofy," Shanti said.

"I'm being honest, Beautiful we all need you, you are our world," Stephon said, turning Shanti's face so she could look at him, her eyes were red and puffy from crying, her eyelids were wet as though more tears were ready to fall. Stephon wanted to cry along with her seeing the woman who never allowed anything to get to her, push through when she was sick and nourished him and everyone else when they were down crying like a newborn baby didn't sit well with him. He was so used to her being able to bounce back within moments but this time she couldn't bounce back as usual.

"Let's pray," he said. If anyone could heal her God could.

"I don't feel like praying right now," Shanti replied.

"How about later on?"

"The way I'm feeling, prayer doesn't work," Shanti said, wiping a single tear from her eyelid.

"What makes you say that?"

"Look Stephon, I don't wanna pray no time soon okay."

"Shanti please don't lose your faith in God," Stephon said.

"Stephon please leave me alone! If you wanna pray, all power to you, but I don't!"

He didn't wanna push her too far he just put his arms around her waist and held her as she drifted off to sleep.

Father God in the name of Jesus heal her heart God, let her know troubles don't last always and let her know you can fill that void in her heart. In Jesus name.

~ CHAPTER ELEVEN ~

Mickie sat quietly on the couch reading a book. Jett opened the door and walked in tossing his lunchbox on the kitchen counter and his backpack and keys on the key rings. He looked over at Mickie and turned his nose up.

"I don't smell no food cooking, I guess I'm gonna be hungry tonight." "You're so worthless," he said under his breath. Trying to say more to himself than to Mickie but she still heard.

"Good afternoon to you too Jett," Mickie responded back closing her book sitting it beside her.

"Don't get smart and get yo teeth knocked out your mouth or thrown out this house again," he snared.

"I didn't get smart with you, and your attitude ain't called for," she stated.

"Who do you think you're talking to?" Jett asked walking into the living room.

"I'm talking to you! I'm so sick of you disrespecting me and treating me like shit! I haven't done anything to you but been good to you," Mickie said pointing her finger in Jett's direction.

"You call how you treat me good? I have to get on to you for you to do simple shit around this place and look it's five in the afternoon and I've worked all day you haven't even prepared any supper," he said.

"Jett, I'm tired."

Jett threw his head back and let out a sarcastic chuckle. "Tired from what? Sitting on yo ass all day gossiping on the phone to your little messy ass home girl or your bougie sister."

"First, of all don't talk about my sister like that she has nothing to do with this and second, there are more ways to be tired than physically."

"I think you're just giving lame excuses," he said.

"Think however you please; I'm not about to argue with you," Mickie said. Mickie had made up in her mind she was going to get her a job and get her life together and never depend on Jett again. Mickie walking towards the kitchen.

Jett walks in front of her and blocks the kitchen entrance. "Don't walk your happy ass in there now. I shouldn't have to tell you what needs to be done."

"I can't win for losing when it comes to you," Mickie said.

Jett grabbed his phone out his pocket and dialed . "Hello…hey what are you up to?"

"Jett, who are you talking to?" Mickie asked.

He waved his hands to hush her.

"No, tell me who you are on the phone with," Mickie asked, standing in front of him and reaching for his phone.

Jett moved out of Mickie's reach.

"Mickie, get out my face before I embarrass you," he muttered moving the phone from his ear.

"Why are you being so rude? What have I done to you?" Mickie asked.

"Mickie, will you shut up and leave me alone!"

"Okay… I'm back… do you want to come over… of course it's fine I wouldn't have asked if it wasn't… bet! See you soon."

Jett moved so closely to Mickie's face she could feel his breath breathing down her throat. "When you go out and get a job and pay one bill in this house then will you have the right to question anything. Are we understood? Until then, keep your mouth shut," Jett said.

Moments later a knock came at the front door and a big smile came across Jett's face. Mickie watched as he nearly ran to the door and swung it open.

"Hey what's up?" Trivia asked, stepping into the doorway. She cannot hide either did she try and hide the look of admiration from Mickie to be honest neither one of them tried. A part of her wanted to walk right up to Jett and slap his taste buds out his mouth but she knew the consequences would be very severe and being homeless was something she could not afford so she just swallowed her pride.

"Do you see this mess? And to top it off she has the nerve to not have any food on the stove," Jett started saying as though Mickie wasn't even in the room. Trivia took a quick glance around and noticed a few dishes in the sink, folded clothes on the sofa and a drink bottle and paper plate on the living room table.

"I'll clean it up," Trivia said.

*Oh no you want this is my house. Micki*e wanted to shout at her but knew better than to say anything.

"Excuse me," Trivia said as she attempted to walk past Mickie to go into the kitchen.

Trivia cleaned the kitchen and placed the dishes and silverware in their rightful places. Afterwards she took the pots and pans off the shelves and began preparing supper. The fact she knew where everything went didn't sit well with Mickie. *Jett's trifling ass really does have the tramp in my house.*

"Now that's what a man is supposed to come home to?" Jett said with a smirk.

"Trivia, I have one question for you. Why are you doing this to me? Why are you sleeping with my man behind my back?" Mickie asked, sauntering into the kitchen to get a better look at Trivia and to see her facial expressions.

"I'm not the one that owes you any answers," Trivia responded.

"Oh, yes hell you do trick have you lost the little common sense you had?" Mickie shouted, as her nostrils flared, and her fists uncontrollably bawled up.

"I don't have time for this bullshit," Trivia said, tossing the dish cloth inside the sink and turning around to leave.

"Hold on," Jett said, clenching Trivia by the arm and pulling her closer to him. "Baby, I invited you over here you don't have to leave," Jett said.

"Baby? What the hell?" Mickie shrieked.

"Yes I said Baby. Mickie you should have known it was over. I haven't touched you in months," Jett said.

Mickie looked from Jett to Trivia. She pursed her lips tightly. Mickie refused to allow them see her cry, so she turned her back to Trivia and Jett and walked out the door. As she was walking out, she could hear them talking.

"I thought she would never leave," Jett said.

I gotta get myself out of this bullshit and soon.

Mickie stood in the driveway and dialed Azure's number.

"Hey Mickie, what's up boo?" Azure answered on the second ring.

"Azure, can you come pick me up and take me over to the career center so I can put in some applications?" Mickie asked.

"Sure, let me throw on some clothes and I'll be there," Azure said.

A few moments later, Azure pulled up and Mickie got into the car.

"What's up with this drastic change?" Azure quizzed, looking over at Mickie.

Mickie looked over at Azure and at first glance she could tell her best friend had threw on something quick to come to her rescue. Azure was wearing a black t shirt with Tupac Shakur face on it and a pair of denim pants, her hair was in a bun with a black headband covering the front of her head.

"Azure, I'm so sick of being taken advantage of. That low down dirty nigga feels like he has an advantage over me because I live in his house. I can't keep living my life that way," Mickie said.

Azure reached over and gave Mickie a tight hug. "I am so proud of you Mickie. I stand by you one thousand percent."

"Thank you girl," Mickie said.

Azure put her car into drive and drive off.

~ CHAPTER TWELVE ~

Kendal Gardener sat quietly on the sofa in his small one-bedroom apartment reading his bible and daily morning devotion before preparing for another day at Bale County Nursing Home and rehabilitation center. The message for today was Wait on The Lord, there were two passages of scriptures from the book of Psalms and one from Isaiah that really stuck in his mind.

Wait for the Lord; be strong and let your heart take courage; wait for the Lord! - Psalm 27:14 NIV.

My soul, wait thou only upon God; for my expectation is from him… He only is my rock and my salvation: he is my defense; I shall not be moved. – Psalms 62:5-6. KJV

But they that wait upon the LORD shall renew their strength; they shall mount up with wings as eagles; they shall run and not be weary; and they shall walk, and not faint. – Isaiah 40:31 KJV.

After reading those passages Kendal got off the sofa and got down on his knees. "Father God Lord Jesus, I come to you now humbly as I know how. I first want to say thank You for allowing me to see another day that was not promised to me, a second chance at making my wrongs right. Lord, I don't wanna ask for anything but I just wanna say thank You for being so merciful and saving my soul. I ask that You use me and my life as a living testimony for your goodness. In Jesus name… Amen."

Kendal bounced to his feet and began thanking God. He had come a long way from where he started. Kendal was an ex-drug addict, he cared about no one, not even himself. It was not until late one Sunday afternoon he ran into Pastor Charles Laughlin at the supermarket and Pastor Laughlin introduced him to Christ Jesus he started attending church and seeking the Holy Ghost. Oh, what a Sunday that was when he finally received God's blessing and promise. Life hasn't been perfect since he started this journey of living a life pleasing to Christ, but it has been well worth it.

One thing Kendal did long for and that was companionship of a woman. He has been praying for over a year for God to send him the right woman, but his prayers haven't been answered yet.

"Lord I've been waiting on you and living my life pleasing to you. I know I shouldn't question you but I'm lonely it's been over a year since I've been with a woman," Kendal said aloud, while putting his shoes on for work.

Wait on my timing son! My timing is not your timing.

"Lord I'm trying, but it gets hard sometimes. I keep myself busy with work and church, so I don't think about it too much."

Continue to trust in me and good things will come to you.

Kendal finished getting dressed for work and as he turned to walk out the door peace came over him.

~ CHAPTER THIRTEEN ~

Leaning her head against the headrest and letting out a loud long sigh, Mickie begin reflecting on her life with Jett and how much things had changed between them since they first became a couple. At first, he worshipped the ground she walked on, brought her all kinds of gifts, and showered her with love. She felt like the luckiest woman alive to have such a loving and caring man in her life. All that changed on the night of their three-year anniversary and still now she doesn't know what brought on that drastic change.

As her mind wondered back to that night... she was in the kitchen finishing up his dinner, she had taken the time to prepare all his favorited dishes: baked pork steaks, homemade loaded mashed potatoes and steamed green beans. Also, she had brought his favorite bottle of wine and to top it off she made a homemade cream cheese pound cake.

"He is going to love this," she said smiling at the meal laid out before her.

The morning half of her day was spent shopping for the perfect dress and heels she wanted to look extra cute for him tonight. Looking at the clock above the stove it was only one hour until he would be driving into the parking lot.

After she was showered and dressed, she took a final glance in the mirror, the navy-blue spaghetti strapped dress hugged her curvy body in all the right places it showed the right amount of cleavage to turn Jett on.

"Happy any..." was all she got out before he put his hand up to hush her.

Oh, wow why is he being rude to me? she remembered thinking to herself.

"Okay well I'm home I'll call you back later… okay you too," Jett said ending the conversation.

"Who was that?" Mickie asked.

"Don't do that… I don't be asking to whom you be talking."

"It didn't sound like one of your coworkers," Mickie replied.

Rolling his eyes, he said. "What you got in the kitchen smelling so good?"

"The first thing you going to speak on is the food not my dress."

Jett looked at the dress hugging her curvy body. "You look ight, I'm ready to eat, shower and go to bed."

"Really Jett? You don't even remember what today is do you?" she asked.

"No is it important?"

"Yes, it is! Today is our three-year anniversary!"

"Happy anniversary Mickie," he said in a sarcastic tone.

"Whatever Jett go eat since that's all you care about right now. I spend my whole day trying to look cute for you and prepare you a good meal and this is how you react," she said.

"I will."

"What's gotten into you?" she said.

"I'm unhappy Mickie and I been that way for a while now."

The news felt like a knife ripping at her heart. Why haven't he told her he felt unhappy?

She stormed upstairs not wanting him to see the tears that were falling down her face. After that night things begin to change between her and Jett, he became a distant stranger to her not wanting to look at her or even be intimate with her.

The sound of someone tapping on her window brought her back to the present.

"Excuse me ma'am sorry to bother you, but I was wondering are you Lauryn Laughlin sister?" A tall, muscular, dark-skinned young man asked.

"Yes I am."

"Your Mickie right?"

"Yes. Do you know me?"

"No, I don't, I attend your sister and her husband church, and you favor her a lot. I remembered her saying she has a younger sister named Mickie," he said.

"What is your name may I ask?"

"Kendal… Kendal Gardner."

"Nice to meet you Kendal," Mickie said with a forced smile.

"I can tell you're hurting and bothered by something but if you leave the situation and give it to Christ Jesus everything will fall into place.

See you inside," he said leaving her with that thought.

God I'm not a praying woman but what are you trying to tell me. I need your help and guidance.

~ CHAPTER FOURTEEN ~

It was seven o'clock in the morning Stephon stood over the stove flipping pancakes, sizzling bacon, and sipping coffee when his next to eldest son Xavion found him. "Good morning, Dad."

"Morning, son everything okay?" Stephon asked.

"No sir. I have a question that's been bugging me," Xavion replied.

"What's up?" Stephon quizzed, turning to give him his undivided attention.

"What's wrong with Mama? She hasn't been out of bed all week."

"She's dealing with a lot mentally all we can do is pray for her son," Stephon said.

"Losing Me-Ma taking its toll on her, isn't it?" Xavion asked searching his father's eyes for answers.

Stephon kept a blank expression, he knew his son was looking to him for answers, but he didn't have any. Shanti was a shell of the woman she once was. "The pancakes smell delicious," Xavion said reaching his hand in the plate of pancakes stacked on the counter but was stopped when Stephon moved the plate out his reach. "Wait until everything is done."

"Hey, it was worth a shot," Xavion said shrugging his shoulders.

"Your old man is to swift for you son," Stephon replied.

"On another note, Dad… you know Bron is coming home next week, I was wondering if you were down for catching a baseball game and going out to eat like old times?" Xavion asked.

"That sounds like a plan Zay," Stephon said as a smile slowly came across his face. It was hard to believe his sons still wanted to spend time with him.

"Dad, can I help you finish breakfast?" Xavion asked.

"Sure son."

After breakfast was cooked Stephon fixed Shanti a plate to take upstairs while Xavion put the food in dishes and sat them on the table.

"I'm about to take this upstairs to your mom and I'll let the girls know it's time to come down and eat."

"Okay."

When Stephon walked into their bedroom the curtains were still pulled back and the room was dark.

"Beautiful, wake up and eat," he said softly.

"Put it on the nightstand I'll eat it later," Shanti murmured.

The plate from last night's dinner was still sitting there it looked as though she hadn't eaten a bite.

"Shanti why is this plate still here? And why is it full?" he asked.

"Stephon I'm too weak to eat," Shanti replied, not budging to turn over and make eye contact with him.

"Maybe if you eat you will feel better," he suggested.

"Stephon can you please go and leave me alone?" Shanti snapped.

"No, I'm not going to leave you alone, your kids are worried about you, I'm worried about you. This is not like you, you gotta kick this Baby."

"Don't you think I'm trying? You don't know my pain," she snared raising her voice.

"Oh, I don't know your pain… I lost my father two years ago and my grandmother just nine months ago. I don't know pain. Baby talk to me if not talk to somebody."

"Stephon please go! I don't have the energy right now," Shanti replied through gridded teeth.

"Shanti, it's been almost a month get up and get yourself together," Stephon said.

"Stephon, please leave me alone," Shanti replied as tears begin pouring down her cheeks.

"Baby, I know it's seeming rough right now, but you have to trust in God," Stephon said, rushing to put his arms around her.

Shanti pushed him away. "I don't feel like being touched right now."

"I'm going back downstairs. I'm here if you need me," Stephon replied.

It broke his heart that for the first time since they were a couple, he could not do anything to take her pain away.

"Stephon, wait, come hold me in your arms," Shanti asked softly.

Without any hesitation Stephon jumped in bed behind her and wrapped his arms around her body. It felt good to have her that close to him again. It had been a long time since he felt the warmth of her body against his.

Shanti turned her body so she could face him, placing his hand on her stomach and her hand over his. "I love you baby, I really do. I'm just dealing with a lot right now. I can't get these thoughts out my head."

"What kind of thoughts, Sunshine?" Stephon asked, staring into Shanti's brown eyes.

There was a moment of silence between the two of them before either one of them spoke again. "I blame myself for what happened to Me-Ma," Shanti said, as tears began filling her eyes.

"Sunshine, it wasn't your fault. Why do you feel that way?"

"I wasn't there for her, Stephon. I chose to allow a total stranger to care for her," Shanti said, trying to fight back tears.

"Me-Ma was a strong-willed woman. She didn't want you putting your life on hold for her and those were her exact words you remember?" Stephon recalled.

"Yes, I do but I should have overlooked that and been there anyway," Shanti said.

"You can't beat yourself up, you gotta pick yourself up and go own with your life," Stephon said.

"It's easier said than done," Shanti said.

"Take one step at a time," Stephon added.

Shanti meets Stephon's lips and kisses him gently. The kiss felt so good it had been weeks since they shared a kiss or even touched one another intimately. He put his hands to her cheeks and held her face tightly as he kissed her. "I love you Sunshine."

"I love you too," Shanti said breathlessly. Stephon started kissing her neck and earlobes, soft moans escaped her mouth as she rubbed his back. When he couldn't take it anymore, he pushed her down on the bed. "Stephon, wait… I'm not ready for this right now," Shanti said. "Give me some more time."

"I understand," he said, taking her into his arms. Shanti relaxed her body in his embrace causing him to smile. He kissed the back of her neck before closing his eyes and saying a short prayer for God to heal her broken heart.

~ CHAPTER FIFTEEN ~

The door was not opening fast enough for Harmony Darwin. "C'mon," she shouted, twisting the doorknob. Sprinting into the living room, tossing her backpack against the wall quickly as possible she began shouting to the top of her lungs. "Mama… Mama… Mama"

"Princess, what doing all that yelling for?" Stephon asked peeping his head out the kitchen.

"Hey, Daddy, I'm sorry for yelling but I got the best news today I got to go tell Mama. Where is she?"

"She's upstairs in bed," he replied.

"By the way it smells good in here, what are you cooking?" Harmony asked while giving her father a bear hug.

"I'm making some of chef boy a dad's famous Parmesan meatloaf, homemade garlic ranch roasted potatoes with fresh veggies and dinner rolls," Stephon said. He did a quick twirl around and bow causing him and Harmony to laugh.

"I'm about to go tell Mama my news and I'll be back," Harmony said still laughing at her father.

When Harmony pushed the room, door open the room was dark no kind of life or light.

She walked slowly to her mother's side and tapped her shoulder. "Mama. Are you okay?"

"Hey Princess, what's up?" Shanti asked with her back still to Harmony.

"I got some fantastic news to share with you," Harmony said not trying to hide the excitement in her voice.

"Can you share it with me later? I have a migraine right now," Shanti replied.

"Mama it's really important you are going to love to hear about this," Harmony said.

"Harmony baby not right now," Shanti whined. For a moment neither one of them said a word.

"Mama no disrespect but I know you miss Me-Ma so do I"- Harmony began and paused. "But when I lost my great grandmother, I wasn't expecting to lose my mother too," Harmony said, as tears began to roll down her cheeks.

Shanti sat up in the bed and for the first time in a long time. Harmony realized the woman in bed was not the woman she knew as her mother. Her once flawless caramel skin was pale; her light brown eyes were dark. She was not the full of life person Harmony knew her as.

"I'm sorry Princess, I got a lot going on right now. I want to hear your good news more than anything but now is not the best timing," Shanti said.

Harmony gave her mother one final look before walking out the room.

She stood in the hallway, put her head in her hands and cried softly.

"Jesus, please heal my mama. I need her. I just lost my great-grandmother. I don't wanna lose my mother too." Harmony prayed and cried.

Weeping may endure for a night, but JOY comes in the morning.

Harmony closed her eyes and began thanking God for the answer she needed.

"Princess. C'mere!" Stephon shouted from downstairs.

Harmony dried her eyes and ran downstairs to the kitchen.

"Yes sir," she said.

"Did you tell your mother your good news?" he asked.

"No sir. She has a headache."

"Yeah, I know. She was up half the night bawling her eyes out," Stephon said.

"Daddy, I'm so worried about her. Have never seen her like this before."

"I know, Princess we gotta continue to pray Jesus bring her out this rough time in her life," Stephon said. "On another note, I want you to try a piece of my meatloaf. Tell me what you think."

Smoke was rising from the fork. Harmony blew hard before she tasted the chunk of meatloaf.

"Ummm… this is delish, Daddy!"

"Thanks! Princess. If you like you can tell me your good news," Stephon replied.

"It's something I really wanted to share with Mama first, but I'll tell you." Harmony began then paused to clear her throat. "You are looking at the first African American homecoming attendant of Bale High school in almost twenty plus years," Harmony announced proudly.

Stephon eyes got watery as he pulled Harmony into his arms.

"I am so proud of you Princess! I know why you wanted to tell your mother so badly you are so much like her. She was the first black attendant her freshman year too, the first black homecoming queen in Bale history and the first black valedictorian," Stephon said.

"Oh wow! Go Mama!" Harmony said.

"Go share your good news with your grandparents while I finish supper," Stephon replied.

"Thanks Daddy, I really hope Mama is doing better when it's time to pick out my dress. I don't want to share that moment with anyone else."

"I bet."

Harmony took out her phone to call her grandparents.

~ CHAPTER SIXTEEN ~

Mickie was in heaven as she walked into Logan's Steakhouse and Grill with Jett by her side.

He held her hand and opened the door for her. Although he was not nice to her often but when he was, he made her feel like the most important person in the world.

I guess getting a job was the best thing I could have done. Things are surely looking up for us. Mickie thought to herself.

"How many are in your party?" a bubbly server asked.

"Two," Jett answered.

"Follow me I'll take you to your table," the server said, grabbing two menus from the stack that rested neatly on the table next to her.

"Are you sure you have enough money to pay for us? I do not wanna get embarrassed." Jett whispered in her ear.

"What kind of idiot do you think I am? If I did not have the money, I would not have asked you out," Mickie said.

"Okay just making sure," Jett said.

Mickie and Jett took their seats in the small booth close to the back of the establishment.

"This place is nice. I remember when I brought…" Jett began and stopped.

"When you brought what?" Mickie asked.

"Nothing never mind."

"Jett, I know you're cheating on me, but can you please respect me enough not discuss it in front of me," Mickie replied.

"Mickie nobody's cheating on you. You are just insecure and think stuff in your head," Jett said.

"If I'm insecure it's because of you," Mickie said.

"How's it my fault?" Jett quizzed.

"Jett…" Mickie began and then paused to suck in some air. "Jett, when we first got together you treated me like a queen, you bought me everything I wanted and needed. Somewhere along the line you begin to change and now I feel like I am with a total stranger."

"I haven't changed, you changed you stop doing all the things you did to get me and keep me happy," Jett replied.

"Why didn't you just let me know what I was lacking instead of distancing yourself and cheating?" Mickie asked.

"Mickie, I shouldn't have to go over simple stuff like that with you, as my quote woman you should already know," Jett said.

"I've been the same since we first met almost ten years ago, and you know that."

"No, you are not…you used to keep yourself up. You were one of the finest women in this town. but now you act like you do not care for real," Jett said.

"Every time I put on an outfit or get my hair did in a certain style and color you criticize me. To be honest you criticize me for everything I do," Mickie said.

"Well Mickie, I have one question for you, if I'm so bad why are you still with me?" Jett asked.

"That is an incredibly good question. I guess because after all these years I am still in love with you."

"If you are not going to leave stop complaining," Jett said.

"Jett do you ever plan on marrying me?" Mickie asked.

"I do not know Mickie one day I may consider. Can we order our food I am hungry?" Jett replied.

Mickie nodded her head and looked down at the menu in front of her.

The car ride home was quite between Mickie and Jett. Mickie hated to admit it, but they were slowly growing apart. Her mind drifted to their one-year anniversary.

Mickie wore a white spaghetti strap dress that hugged her curvy body in all the right places and complimented her flawless skin. Her long black hair had a swoop bang on the right side, a bun up top and the rest hanging down in the back. Jet took her to Mira's an Italian restaurant.

"Today is the beginning of the rest of our lives together. We made it to a year," Jett said, as he held her hand and kissed it from across the table.

Jett's phone ringing interrupted her thoughts. She looked at the Bluetooth radio and seen Trivia's name with a heart and emoji face with two hearts appear on the display.

Jett sent the call to voicemail only for her to call right back.

"Hello…" he answered clearing his throat.

"Why you sent me to voicemail?" Trivia asked.

"I'm kind of busy right now," Jett replied.

"You must be with her?" Trivia asked sounding a bit salty.

"Yes."

"I thought you said you were done with her, and you wanted her out your house?" Trivia questioned him.

"Hold on wait a minute… you been talking about me to Trivia?" Mickie asked turning her body in her seat so she could look him straight in the eyes.

"Trivia let me call you back," Jett said hanging up on Trivia. "Mickie, I do not wanna argue with you okay. Yes, I said something to Trivia a while back."

"Is that how you really feel about me?" Mickie asked.

"To be honest I don't know how I feel about you," Jett replied.

"Jett, I need to know where we stand," Mickie stated.

"Mickie if you wanna leave that is fine with me. I do not need you here with me. I pay all the bills on my own anyways," Jett said matter-of-factly.

"That's so cold," Mickie said.

"It's the truth."

"Your day is coming Jett Beverley," Mickie added.

Jett leans back in his seat and laughs.

Mickie looks over at him and does not say a word. *What was the point?*

~ CHAPTER SEVENTEEN ~

Mickie placed her housekeeping cart between a resident's room and her janitorial closet. There was a deep burning from the inside out from her wanting to release her cries, but she knew it was not the correct timing. She looked around to make sure no one was looking before she slipped into the closet and plopped down in the metal folding chair and allowed the cries that were deep down inside her escape.

Jesus is the only answer to your problems. The words of her mother spoke to her as loud and clear as if she were sitting there with her.

"Mama, I need you now like never before," Mickie cried.

Cast all your cares on him for he cares for you. A voice spoke to her.

"God, I need you! Please help me, Lord Jesus! I cannot do this by myself," Mickie wailed, as tears fell down her face.

Silence

"Lord, have I messed up so bad that not even you cannot help me?" Mickie asked.

He heals the broken-hearted and binds up their wounds.

"I am tired of feeling this way Jesus help me. Let your will be done not my will but yours."

There came a knock on the door interrupting her. Mickie wiped her eyes before slightly opening the door and peeping her head out.

"Hey, Mickie, I just came to check on you," Kendal said with a benevolent smile.

Kendal Gardner had become a good friend to Mickie.

She craned her neck so that she could get a better look at him, he was mahogany brown skinned, she noticed he had a low haircut, a freshly neat even shave, and chocolate brown eyes that were mesmerizing. "I'm fine Kendal thanks for checking on me," Mickie said giving him a simper smile.

"Are you okay?" He asked.

"Yeah, I'm peachy."

"No, you are not, I can tell that something is bothering you. What are you doing after work today?" he asked.

"What is today?" Mickie asked.

"Today is Wednesday," Kendal responded.

"I gotta go home and cook supper. My boyfriend gets off earlier on Wednesdays," Mickie said.

"Why don't you come to bible study with me?" He quizzed.

"I don't know," Mickie shrugged her shoulders.

"God is the only answer to your problems," he replied.

Mickie thought back to the words of her mother and the talk she had with God earlier.

"Kendal, you are right. Yes, I will attend bible study with you tonight. What time do you need me to be ready?" Mickie asked.

"I'll be there to get you by six-thirty just give me your address," Kendal said.

Mickie looked into her backpack and grabbed her pen and notebook. She jotted down her phone number and address and handed the paper to Kendal.

"I gotcha I'll be there by six thirty to pick you up. Have a good rest of the day Mickie," Kendal replied with a smile before leaving her to her thoughts.

"Lord, work a miracle in my life please God," Mickie cried.

~ CHAPTER EIGHTEEN ~

Shanti awakened to the rays of sunlight peeking through her bedroom window.

The excruciating pain from her throbbing headache woke her from her sleep but she still did not possess the motivation to get out of bed and take pain medicine.

Closing her eyes, she dived deeper into the sheets.

The alarm went off.

Shanti let out a long groan before turning over on her side and hitting the stop button.

I am not feeling work today.

All she wanted to do was lie in bed all day in her pajamas and sleep.

There was a loud knock on the door.

"Come on," she said.

Stephon walked in, already dressed for the day.

The white shirt went well with his flawless peanut butter complexion. He placed a plate of breakfast in front of her and a tall glass of freshly squeezed orange juice.

"I thought maybe you would like breakfast in bed," he said with a warm smile revealing his deep dimples, they always warmed her heart.

"Thanks, baby but I'm not hungry," she spoke.

"You have not been eating much of anything. You need to put some food on your stomach," he said.

"I'm fine and besides I have a bad headache," she whined.

"Yeah, I bet you do. It is coming from you not eating." He scolded her.

"I don't have an appetite."

"Baby, you still need to force yourself to eat. Before you end up sick."

Shanti shrugged before looking up at a painting.

She watched out the corner of her eyes Stephon walking into the bathroom and coming out with some Tylenol in his hand.

"Here take these," he said.

She tossed the tablets in her mouth before taking a big gulp of her orange juice.

"Thank you."

Stephon bent down and gave her a kiss on her forehead. "Are you going to try and make downstairs today to see Bron?"

"Oh snap! He is coming home today?" Shanti shrieked.

"Bron, will be pulling up any minute now. He said he has some good news to share with us."

"I'll try my best to make it downstairs," Shanti said.

"Please do it because you know he's going to wanna see you up and moving around," Stephon said before turning to leave out the room.

Shanti nodded her head in confirmation.

"Lord Jesus, I have not talked to you in a long time. I have no excuse for that, there are days I wish could just leave this earth and never return. I need a touch a sign from you," Shanti begged.

I will lift up mine eyes unto the hills from whence cometh my help. My help cometh from the Lord which made heaven and earth.

Shanti jumped. She had not heard the voice of The Lord in quite some time.

"Lord, I need to feel your presence like never before."

He gives power to the faint, and to him who has no might he increases strength. but they who wait for the Lord shall renew their strength; they shall mount up with wings like eagles; they shall run and not be weary; they shall walk and not faint.

Tears began rolling down her cheeks, her eyes closed, and her arms were lifted upward. "Lord, I am sorry for doubting you, you are my strength and my refuge in times of trouble. Please Lord Jesus forgive me and restore me in Jesus's name," Shanti cried out.

I already have my child.

Shanti closed her eyes, and she could hear her Me-Ma voice coming to her saying: *Shani girl, stop blaming yourself it was my time to be with the Lord. There was nothing you are anyone else could do to change that. I am happy, I am free.*

Tears began to slide down her cheeks. "I can't help it Me-Ma I miss you so much."

Shani girl you have to walk by faith and not by sight and never forget God's word is lamp unto your feet and light unto your path. Trust in him even when times get tough.

"Thank you, God, for my revelation I promise to put you first from now on."

Shanti tossed back the covers and sat on the side of the bed. For the first time in a long time, she felt joy deep down inside her soul. "Stephon!" She shouted.

His footsteps were loud as he ran up the staircase. When he reached the room, he stood in the doorway for a moment to catch his breath. The sight of him bent down gasping for air caused Shanti to smile. She did not want him to see her smile, so she covered her mouth with her hand.

"What's up?" Stephon asked once he caught his breath.

"C'mere," Shanti said.

Stephon came and sat beside her on the bed.

Shanti leaned over and planted a wet kiss on his lips. She could not deprive herself of his warm touch any longer and wanted to be closer to him. She lifted her face and moved in to kiss him. He wrapped his muscular arms around her waist as she pressed her soft body on his rock-hard chest. As soon as he opened his mouth, his heat united with hers and captivated her as he kissed deepened with each passing moment. Their breathing became heavier as he nibbled on her bottom lip every now and then. His hands went up and down her back, gently stroking her in all the right places and she released a moan that she had been holding in since their lips touched.

"Shhh… the kids are going to hear us," Stephon whispered in her ear in between nibbles.

Shanti pulled away long enough to sashay to the door and close it shut afterwards joining Stephon on the bed again.

"I want all of you Mr. Darwin," she uttered.

She moaned louder when he touched her inner thigh. She felt her juices being released. She felt euphoria as her hands trembled to unbutton his shirt and expose his bulging chest and six-pack. At forty-three years old it was no secret he still worked out daily. She was almost embarrassed when she realized her mouth had involuntarily started to water over a man, she had been with for nearly twenty years.

Stephon smiled knowing he could still turn her on.

For the first time in a long time Shanti and Stephon enjoyed intimacy between each other.

~ CHAPTER NINETEEN ~

"Hey Dad, is Mama, okay?" Xavion asked, once Stephon walked into the living room smiling from ear to ear.

"She is doing fine son," Stephon said.

A few moments later Shanti walked into the living room. She was dressed beautifully wearing a royal blue two-piece dress suit and a pair of black flip flop with heels to match and her long black hair was in a bun. "Rise and shine family," she said.

"Mama!" Three out of four of her children shouted in unison running to her.

"Mama, we missed you so much," Xavion sang, hugging her as tightly as he could.

"I missed you too son and I promise to try and ever let life beat me up that bad again," Shanti said. Shanti walked over to Harmony and threw her arms around her. "Princess I am so sorry I have not been here for you. I am more than ready to hear your good news over lunch and a trip to the mall," Shanti replied.

"I love the sound of that," Harmony said.

"Does this mean Daddy isn't doing my hair anymore?" Six-year-old Londyn asked. Londyn was the youngest of the four children. She was a pretty little girl with shoulder length silky black hair that was in a bushy ponytail. Londyn has a warm caramel complexion and light brown round shaped eyes.

"Yes, unless you want him to, do you want him to?" Shanti quizzed, smiling down at her miniature twin.

"I like the way you do my hair Mama," Londyn answered. "No

defense Daddy." Looking back at Stephon.

"It's offense and none taken kiddo," Stephon said. Everyone laughed.

"I'm about to head in the kitchen and whip up a quick meal before Bron gets here," Shanti replied.

Just as Shanti was heading into the kitchen the doorbell rang. Stephon walked to the door and looked through the peephole. "He's here!" Stephon shouted. Everyone began screaming and jumping in excitement.

Bron pulled his father into a manly hug soon as he landed his eyes on him.

"Hey Dad," Bron said with a smile.

"Hey son, you are looking good," Stephon said, patting him on his back.

"Thanks, you don't look too bad for an old man," Bron teased.

"Watch it," Stephon said playfully hitting his arm. Stephon led the way into the living room where everyone else were waiting patiently to greet him. Instantly Bron threw his arms around his mother. "I love you and miss you so much."

"Same here son," Shanti said, holding on to their embrace.

One by one Bron hugged his three younger siblings.

"Bron, you said you had some good news for us. We can't wait to hear it," Stephon replied.

"Oh yes, I am glad you mentioned that. I made reservations down at Tiffany's to discuss it over dinner," Bron replied. "We need to be heading there now I got someone meeting us there."

Shanti stood in amazement watching her family scramble around to get out the door. A smile slowly came across her face. *These are the moments I missed the most.* She thought to herself.

You are going to make it child trust in the Lord. She could hear Me-Ma tell her. Grabbing her purse, she closed her eyes for a moment and smiled before joining her family outside.

~ CHAPTER TWENTY ~

As she stepped inside the church doors Mickie felt a sudden feeling of relief. *This is where I need to be* she thought to herself. Her mind drifted back to the last Sunday her mother tried encouraging her to attend.

Mickie was lying in bed cuddled up behind Jett his arms was around her she felt like she was in heaven. Her phone began ringing. The embrace felt so amazing she did not want to turn over and answer her phone. "Hello," she answered, groggily.

"Hey Temetria, what you doing still in bed on a Sunday morning?" her mother asked.

"I was asleep Mama, what's up?" Mickie asked.

"I was callin' to ask you to attend service with me this morning," Mama said.

"No ma'am, not today," Mickie replied.

"Temetria, you were raised in the church, but it is your call. When Jesus gets ready for you, he will call you in," Mama said.

Mickie rolled her eyes.

"I love you Mama and I will talk to you later," Mickie said.

"I love you more baby and I will pray for you," Mama said.

"Thank you," Mickie said, ending the call and cuddling her body against Jett's.

"Hey Mickie, would like to sit in the seat beside your sister?" Kendal asked, tapping her arm bringing her mind back to the present.

"Yes sure," Mickie replied. "I'm sorry about that."

"You're good," he said, patting her on her back.

Lauryn threw her arms around Mickie, rocked her back and forth.

"Oh, my goodness! This is such a great surprise I am so happy to see you!" Lauryn gushed.

"Thank you, sis, it's great to see you to," Mickie laughed.

Lauryn and Mickie took their seats while Kendal sit in the chair beside Mickie.

"I am so proud of you Mickie, getting a job and standing on your own two feet," Lauryn said.

"I have a long way to go but I'm going to make it," Mickie said.

"I know you are and if you need me for anything don't hesitate to call," Lauryn insisted.

"Thank you, sis, that means a lot," Mickie stated.

A few moments later Lauryn's husband Charles sauntered in from the side door holding his black bible case and notebook in his hand. When he spotted Mickie, a smile came across his face. As he rushed over to her and helped her to her feet to pull her into a hug. "Mickie, it is so great seeing you," he said.

"Thank you, Charles… I mean Pastor," Mickie said.

"It's okay Mickie," he chuckled.

Winking his eye at Lauryn he made his way to the front of the church.

The projector screen lit up and the scripture Deuteronomy 31:6 appeared on the screen.

"Tonight, I am going to teach on finding strength during the storm. Storms are going to come in our lives. Our lives feel dark and void during seasons of sadness, we often struggle with emotions of fear or loneliness when dilemmas become overwhelming. It is comforting to know God's presence is consistent. Deuteronomy chapter thirty-one and verse six says: *Be strong and courageous. Do not fear or be in dread of them, for it is the Lord your God who goes with you. He will not leave you or forsake you.* It can get overwhelming at times, but we have to believe and trust in God even when times get hard. I want to encourage everyone of you to begin trusting and believing in God when times are good and when times are bad. God is our refuge our strength especially in times of storms. As I close tonight, I pray that you be encouraged and continue to trust in God. One more thing I am so glad to have my sister-in-love sister Temetria better known to everyone as Mickie, among the congregation tonight…" Charles stopped talking for a moment while everyone clapped their hands happy to see Mickie.

A Time to Love

Lauryn reached over and squeezed Mickie's hand.

Charles said a quick prayer for his congregation before dismissing them.

"How did you enjoy service tonight, Mick?" Lauryn asked, pulling Mickie into a hug.

"I loved it and I'll be most definitely coming back," Mickie assured her.

"Thank you for bringing her," Lauryn thanked Kendal.

"You are more than welcome Sister Laughlin. I did what I was led by the spirit to do," Kendal said.

Kendal led the way out the crowd door.

"Thank you so much for bringing me to church tonight," Mickie said once they got to his car.

"You are more than welcome Mickie anytime," Kendal said. He opened the door for Mickie and closed it when she was in and seated. Mickie was in awe she had never had a man open a car door for her. She had only seen Charles do it for Lauryn and Stephon do it for Shanti. She enjoyed her few moments of quietness before going into World War three.

~ CHAPTER TWENTY-ONE ~

Before Mickie unlocked the door to walk inside, she stood at the door closed her eyes and reminisced on the impressive word from the Lord that was received.

Her mind wondered back to how great Kendal had treated her, opening doors, and buying her supper. He was truly a gentleman and something she was not used to… then it hit, her current boyfriend Jett was not the man God had intended for her to spend the rest of her life with.

Baby some folks are meant to be in your life for a season not forever and when their times up you have to let them go. Mickie recalled her mother telling her one cold Sunday morning. Her mother was hand washing collard greens in her sink and Mickie had come over to vent to her about Jett.

In the eight years they have been together Jett has never done anything like that for her and in the back of her mind Mickie knew she deserved to be treated like a lady.

It is up to me to better myself and get myself out this situation. It may be a rough road ahead, but I can do this.

Philippians chapter 4 and verse thirteen says: I can do all things through Christ which strengthens me.

Mickie smiled to herself before unlocking the door and walking inside. Jett was sitting in the dark with his head hanging low and his shoulders slumped over.

He made eye contact with Mickie, and she could tell he had been crying.

"What's wrong with you Jett?" Mickie asked, flopping down next to him.

"Mickie, I'm sorry for how I have been treating you. I haven't been fair to you at all… please forgive me and give me a second chance."

Mickie sucked in some air. "Jett as much as I want to believe you did a whole turn around I can't, because you have done this so many times before," Mickie replied.

"Baby, I'm for real this time," he said.

Baby? Did Jett just call me Baby? Maybe he is trying to change and make things right? Mickie thought to herself.

"Wait a minute… did you just call me baby?" Mickie asked, smiling at Jett.

"Yes Baby, I did."

"Oh, my goodness you haven't called me Baby in a while. I don't even remember this last time you called me baby," Mickie purred.

"Well, that's about to change I can't afford to lose you Baby. Tonight, when you came in with your mind made up and left for church. I knew then I am bound to lose you soon and I can't imagine my life without you. I love you so much," Jett vented.

Mickie placed her hand on the right side of her chest.

"I love you too Jett," she said.

Jett slowly moved closer to Mickie.

Her heart began beating like a bass drum through her chest, the sound was almost deafening to her ears. "What are you doing?" she asked, leaning back.

"I'm trying to kiss you," he chuckled.

For the first time in a long time Jett gave Mickie an enthusiastic kiss. Mickie did not know what to think or how to feel.

God. Is this your will? Are you changing him into the man he needs to be for me? Mickie thought to herself.

Jett pulled away from Mickie for a moment and stared deeply into her eyes. "Temetria Deanna Pearson…" he began and stopped.

"Yes."

Jett reached his hand out and took Mickie's hand into his. "Will you do me the honors of being my wife?"

"Oh my gosh!" Mickie gushed, putting her hand over her mouth.

"Yes… yes… yes… I will marry you!"

Thank you, God! I knew you would work things out for us. Mickie thanked God to herself.

Jett pulled Mickie into his arms and began hugging and kissing her.

~ CHAPTER TWENTY-TWO ~

Sha'Bron Darwin have always been a moral and ethical young man. He was raised in the church his entire life. At the age of nine he accepted Christ into his heart and though life has given him some twist and turns he never lost his faith. Now age twenty-one he still has those some morals. When he met Laturi James he knew she was the girl for him. The only problem was she didn't have the same Christian upbringings as him.

Bron met Laturi at his first home football game at the University of East Alabama. It was after much praying to God from him, his parents, grandparents, and church family he received a paid scholarship to the university he had dreamed of attending since his freshman year of high school.

It was the night of his first football game his coach, Coach Delroy Brunson was a kind willowy gray-haired man. It was right before the game he asked the gentlemen to join hands and pray.

"Father God Lord Jesus, I ask you to take care of these young men while they're on this field tonight, give them the strength, courage, and attitudes they need to face their opponents and let them know that a win is great, but a loss is also okay too. Please allow no hurt, harm, or danger to come to them tonight. In Jesus name I pray amen."

"Amen," the team said in unison, as they grabbed their helmets and ran out the locker room.

"Darwin," Coach Brunson shouted right before Bron walked out.

"Yes sir," Bron said turning around quickly.

"Darwin, you are different then a lot of these young men on this team I see something in you, always keep your head up and your eyes on God," Coach informed him.

"Yes, Coach and thank you."

Bron hurried towards the field to catch up with his teammates but as he turned the corner to walk into the football field, he ran into someone.

"I'm so sorry," he said.

"You need to watch where you are going," the young lady said with a lot of sass.

"My bad dang," Bron said.

"You good just from now on watch where you're going," she said.

"By the way, I'm Sha'Bron everyone calls me Bron. May I ask your name?"

"I'm La Tour-Rie, and everyone calls me Tour-Rie… nice to meet you Bron."

"Thank you same too you… I gotta hurry on the field but I hope to see you again around campus," Bron said.

Laturi giggled. "Same here, but in a different way not you nearly knocking me over," she giggled.

Laturi was a beautiful young woman, she was petite and flamboyant, flawless cocoa complexion, chestnut brown eyes, full lips, and an hourglass shape.

After the game she was waiting for Bron by the locker room doors.

"I was wondering if you would like to grab a bite to eat?" Laturi asked.

"I would love that, but it's against my religious beliefs to go out unchaperoned," Bron told her.

"What kind of bologna is that!" she shrieked.

"You are a grown man, you can do whatever you wanna do," she said.

"That is true, but I still have my beliefs and that's not going to change. Now I can ask my coach if he and his wife would like to join us. If not, we can't go," Bron stated firmly.

Laturi thinks for a moment and finally she agrees.

Coach Brunson and his wife Mrs. Meredith didn't hesitate to go eat with the two young people. After that night Bron and Laturi became inseparable although his religious beliefs were a problem at times Laturi began to respect them.

A couple of weeks ago Bron decided it was time to pop the big question, but he didn't want to do so without his parents and grandparents blessing.

As he turned into the restaurant parking lot, he looked over at his father sitting quietly in the passenger seat. "Daddy, I have a quick question for you?"

"What up?" Stephon asked.

"At what point in your relationship with Momma did you know she was the one you wanted to spend the rest of your life with?" Bron asked.

There was a moment of silence before either of them spoke a word.

Stephon rubbed his chin and looked over at his son. "To be honest with you son, I knew from the moment I laid eyes on her. She was different and well mannered, she seen me for who I was nothing more and nothing less. Why did you ask me that son?"

"Well to be real with you, I think it's time for me to pop the question to Tour-Rie," Bron said.

"Oh, wow son that's fantastic! I think you two make a beautiful couple," Stephon said.

"Thanks Dad," Bron said. "I haven't said anything to her or anyone else yet so keep this between us."

"I will son."

Bron's heart was racing when he walked inside Tiffany's with his father and younger brother Xavion following behind. The ladies had made it there a couple minutes prior they were admiring the waterfall.

When his parents made eye contact his father smiled at his mother before walking over to her.

"Hey baby," Stephon said pulling Shanti into his arms and giving her kiss on her lips.

See that is the kind of marriage I wish to have after being married for nearly twenty years. Bron thinks to himself.

Before he sauntered to the front desk to speak to the hostess.

"Good afternoon, ma'am, I made reservations for a family of ten," Bron said with a smile.

"Can I get the name the reservations are under?" the young lady asked.

"Yes ma'am. Darwin."

The young lady began typing something on her computer screen before looking back up at Bron.

"Yes, sir right this way," the young lady said.

"Give me just a sec to get my family," Bron said, walking over to the bench and beaconing for everyone to follow him.

Once everyone was seated at the table and his grandparents greeted him.

"I am so happy to see you," Lauryn said giving her eldest grandson a hug.

"Same here," Bron said.

"So am I, you are looking good," Charles said.

"Thank you, Papa," Bron said.

A few moments later Laturi walked in with her parents. Her parents were nothing like Bron's mother and father. Laturi's mother wore a midnight blue spaghetti strap shirt revealing ample cleavage, and a tattoo of a butterfly on her the right side of her breast, a mini black skirt with ruffles at the bottom. She had a pecan complexion, long down to her buttocks burgundy wig, long eyelashes, her face was covered with makeup and she had oval shaped light brown eyes and a delicate nose. They took their seats. Once everyone had finished introducing themselves Bron stood to make his announcement.

"First, I would like to thank everyone for coming out tonight. I have something I would like to ask La Tour-Rie with all of you present," Bron said.

"I wonder what it is?" Stephon said shooting Bron a wink.

"La Tour-Rie James, the last two years have been amazing. I would like to take our relationship to the next level... will you do me the honors of being my wife?" Bron quizzed.

Chants and claps came from the table.

"Yes! Yes!" Laturi shrieked jumping up from her seat and running over to Bron and hugging him.

"I love you so much Sha'Bron Darwin," she cooed.

"I love you too," Bron said.

While their families continued to chant and clap for them.

~ CHAPTER TWENTY-THREE ~

Laturi James and her mother Nadia walked inside Andy's bridal shop to look at a couple of potential wedding dresses for her big day

"What kind of dress do you have in mind?" Nadia asked as they stepped inside.

"I was thinking maybe a trumpet or mermaid dress," Laturi answered.

"Ooh I think that will be beautiful on you," Nadia assured her.

"Thank you, Mama," Laturi said.

Nadia surveyed the room and located the bridal jewelry section. "I'll be back in a sec," she said to Laturi as she hurried to scan over the selections,"

A diamond necklace with the matching earrings caught her eye. She grabbed the set and walked back over to where Laturi was checking out a white velvet dress with sequins going down and a long train that looked like a pool at the bottom.

"What do you think Mama?" Laturi gushed over the dress.

"I love it… and this jewelry set will go right along with it," Nadia replied.

"I don't wear jewelry anymore remember," Laturi reminded her.

"Oh yeah I forgot you gotta fit into Sha'Bron's world," Nadia said sarcastically.

"Mama how many times do I have to tell you my walk with God has nothing to do with Bron. The only thing Bron did was introduced me to Christ the rest was my choice. You should be happy your daughter is choosing to live for Jesus," Laturi said.

"I don't get into that church mess," Nadia replied.

"Maybe you should God is the only one who can help you and he can really help with your… never mind," Laturi shake her head.

"Go ahead Tour-Rie help with what?" Nadia asked.

"I don't wanna argue today," Laturi said.

"Un huh… I'm sorry I'm not perfect like your soon to be mother-in-law," Nadia spat.

"Mama it's not like that me and Daddy have been trying to get you help for years."

"I don't need help!" Nadia raised her voice. She looked around to make sure nobody was hearing the conversation she was having with her daughter.

"Yes you do Mama," Laturi said.

"I can handle my liquor and besides help is for punks I'm no punk," Nadia said folding her arms across her chest. "End of discussion."

"Oh, you don't need help? I can count on all my fingers, toes, and some how many times you have left for days or even weeks at a time leaving me and Daddy to fend for us," Laturi spat, raising her eyebrows, and batting her eyes to fight against the tears that were trying to flow down her cheeks.

"I see you can't let shit go can you? It's like I told your father it's my life and my business what I do," Nadia fired back, pointing her finger in Laturi's direction. Her eyes grew big and red. The blood in Nadia's veins was boiling.

"Mama that is beside the point you need help. I worry that one day I'm gonna get a phone call that something bad happened to you," Laturi stated.

"Girl ain't nothing gonna happen to me," Nadia brushed Laturi off rolling her eyes.

"What about all those times you passed out in other people's houses or passed out in the street, and someone had to bring you home? I am so afraid that one of these days someone is going to take advantage of you in that state of mind or worse kill you. Mama I'm not trying to control you or anything I just want the best for you," Laturi explained.

"Whatever Tourie? I don't have to stand here and take this bull from you. Since your future mother-in-law is so perfect let her help you find your perfect dress," Nadia said throwing the jewelry set on top of the jewelry display table and storming out the bridal shop.

Jesus her life is in your hands please save her from her addiction before it's too late. Help her get to the root of the problem.

Laturi wiped her eyes before putting on a fake smile like she's done so many times before and continued looking for the perfect to become Mrs. Darwin.

~ CHAPTER TWENTY-FOUR ~

Stephon turned off the water and opened the shower door. For a moment he admired Shanti from where he was standing. She looked enticing in her purple satin nightgown, hugging every inch of her body. Soon any thoughts of time and getting ready for bed left his mind as he grabbed his towel from the towel rack and climbed out of the shower. Stephon couldn't help himself, moving behind Shanti to wrap his arms around her and kiss the nape of her neck. He moved in behind her, knowing they fit like a glove and always have.

"Ummm… you smell so darn good," he whispered in her ear, inhaling the natural scent of her skin.

"Thank you… it's called dial soap," Shanti giggled.

Shanti was wiping condensation from the mirror revealing a vision of beauty that he wasn't even sure she herself was aware she possessed. It was something about seeing her, standing there hair in a bonnet, face natural and new made him want her even more but he knew the duties and responsibilities of life called them. Tomorrow morning was going to be the first day back to work for both of them.

She smiled towards the mirror. "I know what's on your mind Mr. Darwin and the answer is no. I need to get to bed I have a busy day ahead of me tomorrow and so do you."

"I know but you are so darn beautiful," he groaned.

"Thank you," Shanti blushed.

Stephon twirled her around to face him and then bent down and give Shanti a wet kiss on her lips. "I love you," he said.

"I love you too," Shanti said.

Stephon gave Shanti one more kiss on her lips before turning to walk into the bedroom. Once he was in bed under the covers Shanti joined him.

"Stephon, I wanna say thank you for how you stayed by me when I was dealing with my mental breakdown," Shanti said.

Stephon sat up straight resting his head against the headboard. "Baby you are more than welcome. When we spoke those vows before God and our families we made a lifelong commitment that I plan to never easily break," he replied.

Tears began to form in Shanti's eyes. "How did I get so lucky to have you?"

"God knew what we both needed in our lives," Stephon stated, kissing her forehead.

"You are right about that, and I hope and pray he blesses Bron union the same," Shanti said.

"I do too, I can't believe my oldest son is getting married soon. It seems like yesterday he was begging me to play basketball in the backyard after work," Stephon recollected.

"Times flies when you're having fun," Shanti said.

Shanti and Stephon got out of bed and got down on their knees, holding hands from opposite sides of the bed and began praying to God.

~ CHAPTER TWENTY-FVE ~

Jett was exceptionally nice to Mickie before work.

"Good morning, baby," he said with a smile.

Mickie walked into the kitchen breakfast was already laid out on the table: grits, scrambled eggs, patty sausages and homemade cinnamon toast and to wash it down a tall glass of apple juice her favorite.

"Good morning, it smells delicious, and it looks delicious as well," Mickie gushed.

"Thank you I wanted to make sure you went to work on a full stomach," he responded.

Mickie sat down and before long Jett joined her.

"What time do you have to leave for work this morning?" Mickie inquired.

"I don't have to work today I'm going to stay home and do some work around the house to make it easier on you," Jett informed her.

"Awesome! I appreciate that," Mickie said.

"I want us to work. I really do love you and I want you to be my wife," Jett assured her.

Mickie looked up at Jett and smiled.

"I want us to work too. I'm tired of all the fussing and fighting and most importantly I'm ready to get married I'm tired of living in sin," Mickie added.

"I feel you," Jett said.

After they finished eating Jett washed up the dishes while Mickie dried them.

"What why are you smiling so hard?" Jett asked.

"It's been a long time since we been together enjoying each other like this. I feel like I'm in a dream," Mickie said.

Jett reached across the table and caressed Mickie's hand. "I promise to make every day like this from now on."

"I like the sound of that Jett Beverley," Mickie replied.

Jett looked down at his phone. "It's about time for you to head to work."

"Yeah I know. I'll give you a call on my breaks," Mickie said rushing to the door.

"Gone ahead and talk to your friends I plan to stay busy the whole day," Jett said. He walked Mickie to the door and gave her a kiss on the lips. Jett stood in the doorway and watched until Mickie drove off.

~ CHAPTER TWENTY-SIX ~

Shanti walked onto the threshold. "Ooh wee! Thank you Jesus I'm finally home!" She said to herself as she unlocked the door and walked into the living room. She placed her car keys on the key ring along with her purse. Before stepping on the soft carpet floor, she took off her seven in a half size heels one by one and placed them by the door.

No one was home to interrupt her, so she headed for the bedroom to do some online charting she didn't finish during the day. When she logged on to the desktop she realized the browser had been recently opened.

"I wonder what Stephon been looking up?"

Shanti clicks on the browser and sees three porn sites that had been visited.

"What in the world?" Stephon knows this is wrong."

Shanti sat at the computer contemplating on how she was going to address him with this issue.

Had it really come to this was he so bored with me that he had to look at other women? Shanti thought to herself. Shanti thought to herself for a moment during the time she was grieving over her grandmother had her husband turned to watching porn to satisfy his needs.

Stephon walked into the room bringing her mind back to the present.

"Hey Baby," he said giving Shanti a kiss on the cheek.

"We need to talk," she huffed not giving any second thoughts.

Stephon plopped down on the foot of the bed. "What's up?"

"I'm going to get straight to the point… why are there porn sites on this desktop?" Shanti pointed to the computer screen.

"I don't know… I don't watch porn. I know it's a sin," Stephon said. "And besides I don't need porn to get me in the mood." Stephon put his arms around Shanti's waist trying to lighten her attitude.

"I'm being serious right now," Shanti said.

"Baby, I don't know one of the boys was probably watching it. Bron and I are having dinner and discussing wedding plans and I gotta pick Xavion up from football practice afterwards. I'll talk to them both," Stephan informed her.

"Thank you," Shanti replied.

"No problem… how was your first day back to work?"

"It was actually pretty good except Cassie kept asking me was I okay," Shanti replied.

"She's just worried about you and making sure," Stephon added.

"I know I'm thankful to have friends who care."

Stephon gave Shanti a kiss on the lips before walking into the bathroom. Shanti followed Stephon into the bathroom. "I was really worried you had gotten bored with me and started watching those videos to satisfy you were I was not able to," Shanti said.

Stephon looked into the mirror at Shanti. "Baby, you are the most beautiful woman in the world to me I can never get bored with you, you are my forever love," Stephon reassured her.

"Awe, thank you Babe. I love you too," Shanti gushed.

~ CHAPTER TWENTY-SEVEN ~

Stephon was sitting on the couch watching some football clips of Sha'Bron back in high school thinking to himself where had the time gone. It seemed just like yesterday Stephon was a junior in college finding out that his girlfriend a sophomore Shanti Laughlin was pregnant with his son. He remembered how afraid both of them were when they first found out Shanti was pregnant with Sha'Bron. Stephon tried to be brave for her, but he was scared too because he didn't know anything about fatherhood, but he knew he loved her and wanted to spend the rest of his life making her and their child happy

"Hey Daddy, are you ready to head out?" Sha'Bron asked, interrupting Stephon's thoughts.

"No son, not quite have a sit I need to discuss something with you."

Bron ambled over to the opposite couch and sat down. "What's good?"

"I'm going to get straight to it your mother bought it to my attention she found open porn websites on the desktop this afternoon. Do you know anything about that?" Stephon queried.

Bron dropped his head. "Yes sir it was me."

"Do you care to talk about why you were looking at porn sites?"

"I'm ashamed to admit it I am a twenty-one-year-old male and still a virgin. I'm getting married in a few months and I want to please my future wife, but I haven't had any prior experience. I don't want her to laugh at me or get bored with me," Bron stated.

"Son, you don't have to worry about anything like that Tour-Rie is marrying you because she's in love with you. Matthew 19:6 says So they are no longer two but one flesh. What therefore God has joined together, let no man separate. You are doing things the way God intended he is going to bless your union," Stephon said.

"Thank you Daddy I'm so worried," Bron admitted.

"Don't be son remember what God joined together no man can separate. You are doing things pleasing to God," Stephon informed him.

"Yes sir thanks. Are you ready to get this night started," Bron asked.

"Yep! Have you guys set a date yet?"

"Yes June nineteenth it's a special date to me," Bron said.

"Oh yeah what's so special about that date?" Stephon asked.

Sha'Bron eyes got big as he stared at his father. Stephon knew this date must be something special from the way Sha'Bron stared at him.

"Daddy, you don't remember what happen on that date?"

"No, I honestly don't," Stephon said.

"You married Mama that exact date in two-thousand and four," Sha'Bron reminded Stephon.

Stephon's heart skipped a beat. How could he forget the day he married his best friend, the love of his life.

"Oh shoot! I forgot I gotta make sure I plan something special for your mother right after your wedding is over. Thanks for reminding me!"

"How about you guys do something fun the week after my wedding, so you guys don't be so tired and overwhelmed. You guys can enjoy one another's company better," Bron suggested.

"Great idea son!" Stephon said.

"Your welcome," Bron chuckled.

"We have a lot of planning to do," Stephon said while walking out the door.

~ CHAPTER TWENTY-EIGHT ~

Trivia was in her kitchenette preparing a quick lunch for herself. Then someone rang her doorbell. "I wonder who's at my house this time of day?" she said aloud. "Just a minute," she shouted. Trivia grabbed her decorative kitchen towel and wiping her hands before walking into the living room to see who was at the door.

She opened the door and looked into the eyes of Jett. "Hey there, what are you doing here?" she asked.

"It's been a few days since I seen you and wanted to see you," Jett said smiling at her.

"Awe isn't that sweet," Trivia replied.

"I also wanted to give you this," Jett said reaching into his pocket and handing Trivia a fist full of money. "Go have a fun day, get your nails, toes or whatever done."

"Thank you, Babe!" Trivia purred jumping into Jett's arms and hugging him.

"Anything for my favorite girl," Jett said pulling her into his arms and kissing her lips passionately.

"Wait… Jett we need to talk," Trivia said.

"What's up?"

"Jett I can't help but think it is more to the story with you and Mickie than what you are letting me know because every time she sees us together, she doesn't act like a woman who's just a roommate but more like a girlfriend. Can you please tell me the truth are you two together?" Trivia glared into his eyes as though searching his eyes for the truth.

"Trivia, everything I ever told you was true. Me and Mickie are no longer a couple. I got tired of her being lazy and not cleaning up and taking care of the house. I moved on with you, but she can't accept that just the other day she asked me did I wanna marry her," Jett said.

"What did you say?" Trivia quizzed.

"I told her hell no the only woman I wanna marry is you," Jett said, rubbing Trivia's hand.

"Awe do you really mean that," Trivia said.

"Yes, baby, you are the only one for me and the only one I need," Jett said.

"When are you going to finally give her that push to get her own spot?" Trivia asked.

"I'm letting her save her money up," Jett said.

"Hey, I have an idea. How about we go grab a bite to eat?" Trivia suggested.

"I don't know about that," Jett said.

"Why not? You have the day off and so do I," Trivia pleaded.

Jett looked at Trivia and seen the sad face she was making.

"How can I say no to that beautiful face. I'll wait while you get dressed," Jett said.

Trivia glanced up at Jett from across the table.

I really hope that everything he's telling me is true. I know it's wrong to go behind a family member or friend that's code, but there's something about Jett Beverley that makes it easy to break all the rules.

Trivia was deep in her thoughts until Jett's phone ringing interrupted her.

"Do you need to answer that?" Trivia asked.

"It's nobody but Mickie and I told her I had things to do today not to be calling me," Jett spat.

Jett's phone kept ringing until he turned it on vibrate.

"Maybe something's wrong," Trivia said.

"Nothing's wrong with her she just wanna aggravate me," Jett rolled his eyes. "This is our time to enjoy one another."

Trivia smiled at Jett. *I guess he is being real with me he chose me over her.*

~ CHAPTER TWENTY-NINE ~

I've been calling and texting Jett for almost an hour. Why isn't he answering his phone or responding back to me? Mickie thought to herself as she turned on the street of their house. She drove up to the carport. Jett's 2021 midnight blue GT mustang was in its usual parking spot. An unfamiliar car was right behind his. It was a silver 2005 Nissan Altima.

"I know good and doggone well Jett is not cheating on me after proposing to me just a few days ago," Mickie said to herself.

Flee away from here! A voice spoke to her. Mickie was determined to see what was happening with Jett.

She reached inside her purse to grab her house key before stepping out her car and walking up the sidewalk. Slowly and quietly, Mickie unlocked the door and walked inside. Taking off her shoes quietly she tip-toed upstairs and when she reached the top of the stairs, she realized the master bedroom door was closed shut.

What is really going on here? She thought to herself.

Without thinking twice Mickie pushed the door open. She stood frozen in total shock. It was as if time had stopped in that very moment. Mickie stood there searching for the words to say but the words would not come out her mouth.

"What the world?" Mickie said when she finally found her voice.

"What are you doing home?" Jett asked pulling the covers over his body.

"Jett how could you, you told me it was over between you and Trivia, you asked me to marry you," Mickie replied as tears spilled onto her cheeks.

"Wait a minute you asked her to marry you? You told me y'all wasn't together and she was getting her own spot soon," Trivia stated.

"Mickie is lying I never asked her to marry me," Jett said.

Mickie looked at him in disgust. "You know what I'm no longer going to allow you to make me look like a fool. Trivia he is all yours I'm out," Mickie said.

Jett jumped out of bed. "Where are you going to go Mickie? I have taken care of you for almost nine years," Jett questioned her.

"I have a job now or did you forget that and a family who loves me. I can stay in my mother's old house my sister has been trying for the longest to get me to move in it. So, I can make it without you," Mickie said.

"So, you think I'm supposed to just let you walk out that door after I've taken care of you and provided for you. Heifer you're my property!" Jett yelled.

"Jett Beverley, you don't intimidate me anymore," Mickie said.

Jett stomped over to his side of the bed and lifted the mattress. He pulled out his turquoise camouflage Taurus 44 magnum. He pointed the gun in Micki's direction.

"Jett put that gun down if she wants to leave let her go," Trivia cried.

"Shut up! This has nothing to do with you!" Jett screamed at Trivia. "Now as I was saying do you think I'm going to let you leave me without any consequences?" Jett asked pulling the hammer back.

Click! Click!

"She's fully loaded and ready to fire so what's it gonna be Mickie?" Jett asked.

Mickie could feel the hair on the back of her neck stand up. Her heart began beating like a bass drum through her chest.

Mickie turned around and tried to run for the door. Jett pulled the trigger and shot her in the back of her left leg.

"AHHHH!" Mickie yelped in pain as fell to the floor in a heap.

"TURN OVER AND FACE ME SLUT!" Jett yelled, his eyes were big, and he was gridding his teeth.

Mickie turned over to face Jett. "Jett please don't kill me!" Mickie pleaded tears rolling down her cheeks.

"To late for that! The only way you are going to walk out my house is if you are in a body bag," Jett shot her again this time on the right side of her jaw.

Trivia jumped off the bed and tried to take the gun from him. Jett hit Trivia in her mouth with the barrel of the gun causing blood to spill out her mouth. Trivia fell to the floor crying. It seemed as though in Mickie's eyes everything was happening in slow motion. Jett squatted down on top of her he got a tight grip around her throat. "I wanna watch you beg me for your life."

Images of her and Kendal discussing she should have stayed at work materialized in Mickie's mind.

"You think you gonna jus leave me?" Jett tightened his grip. A vision of her opening a birthday gift from Jett... "As good as I been to you," he shouted. Mickie seen an image of her mother standing over her crying.

"I made sure you didn't want for nothing!"

Mickie fended off as many of Jett's blows as she could. Breathing was becoming impossible, her body was limp she could feel herself getting weaker, but she refused to give up and let go.

She could hear Trivia crying and Jett yelling for her to hush.

It happened so fast, she thought. *I should have listened to Kendal and stayed at work... God I'm not perfect and I'm not filled with the Holy Ghost please God give me a second chance don't let me be out of time...*

The room dimmed in her view, her surroundings grew darker and darker. Her breathing became labored, and it was soon hard to focus.

God am I alone...

Jett let go of her throat right before she passed out.

Mickie placed her hand around her neck and began wheezing for breath while Jett stood over her and laughed.

"One more thing," Jett told Mickie right before he cocked the trigger back and shot her in between her eyes.

"AAAAAHHHH!" Trivia screamed. Trivia tried to run to Mickie, but Jett grabbed her and pointed the gun towards her head.

"Now are you on my side or hers because if you are on her side. I can blow you brains out right now!"

Trivia closed her eyes and sobbed softly to herself.

"Bring yo ass own," he yelled using one hand to hold the gun to Trivia's head and the other to push her out the door.

Mickie laid on the hardwood floor in a pool of her own blood. Blood was dripping from her face covering the hunter green scrub top she wore; both of her legs were covered in blood as well. Her breathing was shallow as she saw a shadow in front of her. Mickie blinked for a clearer view. It was Kendal. "Hold on Mickie help is on the way." Mickie could feel her life easing away. Kendal fell to the floor beside her, he wrapped her body in his arms.

"C'mon Mickie stay with me," he pleaded.

In the distance sirens could be heard.

"You hear that Mickie the paramedics are almost here," Kendal said.

Mickie opened her mouth to speak but no words came out as she closed her eyes, and her breathing stopped.

~ CHAPTER THIRTY ~

"Jett! How could you treat her like that? You left her laying there in a pool of blood," Trivia gasped.

"Mickie deserved that! I didn't do anything to that ungrateful little... tramp! She thought she was going to use me all these years and just leave!" Jett snapped.

"What did you expect her to do when you did nothing but lied, cheated, and abused her..." Trivia paused for a moment speaking those words made her think. *How could I have been so blind not to see he's been lying to me and her the whole entire time.*

"You brought another woman into the home you two shared. Did you really think she was going to continue wanting to be with you after all that," Trivia stated.

Jett stood from the couch in their hotel room and stormed over to Trivia sitting on the bed. He grabbed her by the throat and began choking her so hard he lift her feet off the ground and pressing her body against the wall. "Let's get something straight I never did anything to Mickie but took loving care of her. She used me until she got on her own feet," Jett yelled digging his claws into Trivia's flesh.

"Jett you're hurting me... I can't breathe," Trivia yelped in pain.

Images of herself at the age of six flashed before her eyes. Her and Mickie were in Me-Ma's backyard having a tea party with their baby dolls and stuffed animals. Another image of herself came to mind age fifteen when her mother died she was carrying a suitcase up the front porch and her social worker had her other belongings bringing her to live with Me-Ma and Mickie. *Lord is this what it feels like before you die? I'm can't hold on much longer… someone save me.* Trivia thought to herself as she began to lose consciousness. With the little strength she had left she looked into the eyes of the man that told her he loved her and wanted to spend the rest of his life with her squeeze life out of her.

~THIRTY-ONE~

It was around 9:00 Pm. When Lauryn's cellphone rang.

"Hello," she answered on the first ring.

"Hey Sister Laughlin, this is Kendal I need you to come to the hospital as soon as possible," his voice was low and deep.

"Is everything okay?" Lauryn asked.

There was a moment of silence on the line.

"No ma'am. It's Mickie, Jett shot her twice and left her for dead. It doesn't look good for her."

"Oh my gosh! I'll be there soon," Lauryn said ending the call.

Lauryn's chin quivered, she struggled to find the words. Charles sat patiently waiting for her to respond.

"Charles, I need to get to the hospital as soon as possible," Lauryn stammered.

"What's wrong baby?" Charles voice was low and soothing.

"It's Mickie, she's been shot," Lauryn struggled speaking the words.

The dream she had a couple weeks prior played in mind. In her dream Mickie was in jail for two accounts of murder but now she got the call Mickie had been shot.

"I'll go grab the keys and meet you in the car," Charles replied.

Lauryn held her hand to her chest nodded her head in affirmation.

When Lauryn walked outside Charles was standing beside the opened passenger door waiting for her with a benevolent smile.

Charles gave her a hug and kiss before helped her in and closed the door and walked to the driver's door.

"Before we leave home let's pray and ask God to heal, deliver and save Mickie," Charles instructed.

Charles and Lauryn joined hands.

"Father God Lord Jesus, we come to you now humbly as we know how. I first wanna say thank you God for our lives, health, and strength. Thank you for our family, friends, and church families. Next God I ask you to heal Mickie's body, mind and soul set her free from the chains of life, the chains of the enemy and the things that have her bound. In Jesus name. God go into the hospital room and heal her body in Jesus holy name I pray amen."

"Amen."

"I trust and believe God is going to work it all out," Charles replied.

"Me too," Lauryn said softly.

Charles drove to the emergency room entrance and parked the car. "Baby, God is going to pull Mickie through."

"I believe he is too. I can't help but wonder what was going on so bad in her life that she couldn't come to me?" Lauryn cried.

"You know how Mickie is she didn't want you worrying about her," Charles soothed her.

"She's my little sister all I have left from Mama. I can't lose her Charles."

"I know Baby." Charles put his arms around Lauryn and held her as she released her tears.

A few moments later Lauryn stepped out of the car and walked towards the entrance. Her heart was beating rapidly. *God I just lost my mom less than six months ago please don't take my little sister away too.* Lauryn thought to herself. Lauryn walked to the front desk there a dark-skinned woman sitting there looking down at something on her phone.

"Excuse me," Lauryn addressed her.

"Yes ma'am. How may I help you?"

"I am here to see Temetria Pearson…" was all Lauryn got her mouth before Kendal ran up to her to show her to Mickie's room. Kendal looked tired and broken-hearted. "Are you alright?" Lauryn asked.

"No ma'am I'm not. I am so worried about Mickie," he said.

"I know all we can do is pray for her," Lauryn reassured him.

"Come on let me take you down the hall to her room," Kendal replied.

Lauryn walked behind Kendal as he walked slowly in front of her.

They reached a room on the right side of the hallway. Kendal turned around facing Lauryn with a sincere look and pain in his eyes. "Sistah Laughlin, brace yourself Mickie doesn't look the way you seen her last."

Lauryn nodded her head in agreement. *Lord how bad did my sister get shot?* Lauryn thought to herself. She held her head heavenward. *I will lift up mine eyes unto the hills, from whence cometh my help. My help cometh from the Lord which made heaven and earth.* Afterwards she released a deep sigh before strolling into her younger sister's hospital room. Lauryn put her hand over mouth and let out a loud horrifying cry she almost dropped to her knees. Kendal rushed to her side hugging her. The image was too much for her to bear Mickie's head was swollen so bad it looked unreal something similar to a gigantic ball placed on a human body. Her eyes were black, blue, and swollen. Lauryn could not see her mouth the respirator covered it, but Lauryn could tell Mickie's lips were swollen as well. The same small chest Lauryn had watched inhale and exhale so many times before now struggles and has to have help.

Slowly, with Kendal's help guiding her steps Lauryn walked over to her bedside.

"How… how… could Jett hurt her like this?" Lauryn cried out. At that very moment Lauryn could not help herself she felt hatred towards Jett Beverley for putting her sister in the position. Lauryn covered Mickie's hand with her own. "Mickie I am so sorry this happened to you. I wish I would have been a better sister to you instead of judging you I should have protected you." Kendal sat in the corner blinking back his tears. "Why didn't I try harder to make her stay at work today? I could have protected her from him."

"Don't beat yourself up, you didn't know this was going to happen to her," Lauryn spoke softly. "Mickie just got to pull through this. I don't know what I'd do if something happened to her," Kendal said. Through her tears Lauryn smiled at Kendal. "You have feelings for her don't you?" Kendal nodded his head in affirmation. "More than you can imagine," he uttered.

A couple moments later a short petite nurse with blonde hair and blue eyes walked into the room. "Good evening, my name is Kayla. I am Miss Pearson's nurse for tonight. How's everybody doing?" she asked in a strong southern accent.

"I've been better… How are you?" Lauryn asked.

"I'm okay you must be her older sister this young gentleman was referring to," Kayla said looking in Kendal's direction.

"I am," Lauryn said with a forced smile.

Kayla looked at the charts before speaking again. "Do you mind this gentleman hearing Ms. Pearson's information?" Kayla asked.

"I don't mind at all," Lauryn said without hesitation.

Just as Kayla was getting ready to start reading over Mickie's chart Charles walked into the room and rushed to Lauryn's side. Kayla takes a deep breath before she begins speaking. "After going over Ms. Pearson's chart test result came back she has some brain trauma we don't know how bad at the moment not until more test are ran. There is swelling on her brain and from what was seen from her cat scan there is a small piece of skull shattered. The doctors and I are doing everything we can to keep her stable and comfortable. Tonight, is going to be extremely difficult for her if she pulls through tonight she will be in the clear somewhat, but she still has a long healing process," Kayla informed. "I'm going to leave you all for a moment and I'll be back to check-in later." Kayla gave Lauryn a hug and shook Kendal's and Charles' hands before exiting out the room pulling the door up behind her.

"Charles why did I have to always be so judgmental about everything she ever did? I was supposed to been there for her and be her older sister. Now my baby sister is fighting for her life… I just lost my mother I can't lose my baby sister too," Lauryn started sobbing on Charles' shoulder.

"Baby you were doing what you felt was right, we never can estimate the depraved thoughts going through someone's mind," Charles appeased her while stroking her back up and down.

"I could have been a better sister, when God heals her and brings her home I'm going to be the best older sister I can be."

"I almost forgot I called baby girl while I was in the car her and Stephon are coming to visit Mickie sometime tomorrow after they finish with Bron and Princess," Charles appraised.

"Okay I think I am going to spend the night with Mickie tonight. So, I'll be here if she wakes up or needs something," Lauryn replied.

"You and Pastor go ahead and go home and y'all get some rest I'll stay here with Mickie," Kendal spoke up.

"Are you sure Kendal? You have done so much today," Lauryn replied.

"Yes ma'am. Go home and rest up so you can be well rested

tomorrow," Kendal added.

"You are such a blessing. Thank you," Lauryn said.

"This means a lot to us," Charles chimed in.

"You guys are more than welcome," Kendal smiled.

Lauryn walked over to Mickie's bed and leaned down to give her a kiss on her forehead. "I love you, baby sister more than you could ever know," she whispered in Mickie's ear.

Charles walked to Mickie and placed his hand over her forehead uttering a silence pray for her. He kissed her cheek. "You are going to be healed and have an amazing testimony," he whispered.

Charles put his hand in Lauryn's hand. "Thank you again brutha."

"If anything changes I'll give you guys a call," Kendal said.

"Thank you so much," Lauryn said giving Kendal a quick hug before walking out the door.

~THIRTY-TWO~

After Lauryn and Charles said their goodbyes to Kendal and Mickie. They walked out the room and pushed the door up behind them. Kendal flopped down on the recliner beside the bed, leaning over enough to reach Mickie's hand. He placed his hand in her hand. "Mickie I am so sorry this happened to you, you didn't deserve this. If only I would have talked with you a little longer and encouraged you to stay at work you wouldn't be laying in this hospital fighting for your life now," Kendal said blinking back tears. "I'm sorry I failed you."

It had been a long time since Kendal Gardener cared this much about a woman and it almost scared him.

Lord what's came over me? Why does Mickie have this effect on me? Kendal thought to himself as his mind wondered back on his past relationship with his ex-fiancé Deena. In the beginning everything was perfect they loved one another so he thought, but something happened along the way that caused her to have second thoughts and leave him at the altar. That day when she humiliated him in front of his family and friends Kendal vowed to never love again but it's something about Mickie he can't seem to shake. Kendal caressed her hand.

Lord is she my one? Is she the woman you created for me to spend the rest of my life with? Kendal thought to himself. Kendal recounted a Wednesday night a few weeks back after bible study him and Mickie went to eat pizza at his favorite pizza restaurant Pablo's Pizza and More.

"Do you like pizza?" He asked turning into the parking lot.

"What kinda question is that everyone loves pizza," Mickie replied.

"I don't know I'm just asking," he shrugged his shoulders.

Kendal stepped out his car and walked over to the passenger door and opened it for her.

He remembered how her eyes would light up every time he opened her door for her. It would always bring a smile to his face to see her light up.

"What's your favorite toppings?" he asked as they walked inside.

"I'm a meat lover type of chick," Mickie giggled.

"Oh really? I am too."

Kendal ordered them a large pizza, a pasta dish, salad, and drinks before sitting at a booth and enjoying her good company. *How could someone purposely hurt such a beautiful person? I would love the chance to have a beautiful and caring woman like Mickie in my life.* Kendal thought to himself glancing down at her.

Trust in the Lord with thine heart and lean not unto thine own understanding. In all thy ways acknowledge him and he shall direct thy paths The scriptures Proverbs 3:5-6 played in his mind.

Lord what are you trying to tell me? Kendal asked himself.

Open your heart and forgive my child. First John chapter four and verse eighteen quotes: There is no fear in love; but perfect love casteth out fear because fear hath torment. He that feareth is not made perfect in love.

Kendal looks heavenward and speaks aloud to himself. "God had not given me the spirit of fear but of a sound body and mind. I will no longer allow my past to hold me back from what God has in store for me." At that moment, all the baggage of his past he had been carrying around Kendal let go. With tears rolling down his face he glanced at Mickie and massaged her forearm. "Mickie, you got to pull through this. I love you; I promise you; you pull through you will never have to worry about being hurt or mistreated again because I am going to protect you with my own life," he vowed to her. "Come on fight for me fight for us Mickie."

~THIRTY-THREE~

Laturi laid on her stomach stretched out across her queen-sized bed with her headphone over her ears listening to an audiobook on her cellular phone. Until her phone started playing K-Ci and JoJo Hailey's "All My Life." "Hey, you," Laturi answered soon as the song began playing over the audio. She was smiling from ear to ear.

"Hey, yourself, you sound exultant to hear my voice," Sha'Bron teased with a soft chuckle.

"I'm always exultant to hear your voice," Laturi replied.

"I am so happy to hear that. What are your plans for the next half hour?" Sha'Bron asked.

"Nothing that I know of I'm just laying her listening to an audiobook," Laturi said.

"Oh really? What's the name of the book?" Sha'Bron asked.

"It's Time to Heal" by a female author named Karyn Kinderson. She writes Christian love novels," Laturi informed him.

"It sounds interesting," Sha'Bron said.

"You have no idea!" Laturi sang.

Sha'Bron chuckled. "Tour-Rie, I was wondering if I could come over. We can talk, go over wedding plans, and grab a bite to eat later on?" Sha'Bron asked.

Laturi's heart started to beat rapidly. The whole two year she's been dating Sha'Bron he has never been to her house.

"I don't think that's a good idea," Laturi said.

"We are going to be married in less than four months when am I going to see where you grew up?" Sha'Bron asked.

It was nothing amazing about where she grew up. She thought to herself.

"In due time I'll show you where I grew up and why can't I just come to your parents' house like I normally do?" Laturi queried.

"No one is home right now you know how I feel about us being completely alone," Sha'Bron said.

"Yes, I know," Laturi let out a deep sigh.

Lord I really do wanna see Bron, but I know for a fact my Momma is in the living room passed out on the couch drunk. Laturi thought to herself. "You can come over my Momma is home," Laturi said.

"I'll be there in a few minutes," Sha'Bron said before hanging up.

Laturi leaned her head against the headboard. "Jesus please don't let Momma embarrass me in front of Sha'Bron," she prayed aloud.

Laturi sashayed into the living room the first thing she noticed was her Momma's feet dangling over the arm of the couch. She walked in front of the couch to get a full view of her mother laying on the couch. Laturi's mother had an empty bottle of alcohol on the coffee table and beer bottles scattered all over the table as well.

"Momma, wake up," Laturi yelled loud enough for her mother to hear.

"What are you doing all that yelling for?" her mother asked sitting up and stretching her arms and legs out.

"Sha'Bron is on his way over here can you please go put on some decent clothes and act with some common sense?" Laturi asked.

"I'm a grown woman and I'm your momma you don't talk to me like that Tour-Rie," her mother slurred.

Tears of un describable pain formed in Laturi's eyes. "Momma if you embarrass me, I'll never forgive you," Laturi declared.

"I don't see why you wanna be with some wannabe pro ball player when you could marry a lawyer or something," her mother added.

Before Laturi could say anything, the doorbell rang. Laturi took a deep breath before walking slowly to the door and opening it.

"Hey Tour-Rie," Sha'Bron greeted soon as Laturi opened the door.

"Hey Bron," Laturi giggled. "Come on I'll show you around the house." Laturi took Sha'Bron by the hand and led the way into the living room.

"Hey Ms. Nadia, how are you today?" Sha'Bron kindly greeted Laturi's mother.

"Hey Bron," she slurred.

Laturi placed her hand in Sha'Bron's hand and walked down the hall to her room. "This is my room when I come home to stay."

Laturi didn't like to come home often being away in college was her time away from her mother and her drinking addiction. There had been times when her mother would become abusive towards Laturi and her father.

Laturi's mind drifted back to the last night she had spent at home with her parents it was the night after she turned eighteen.

Her mother had gotten wasted at Laturi's birthday party. She ended up embarrassing Laturi in front of all her friends by starting a fight with Laturi and physically abusing her. Something in Laturi's brain clicked that night while she was in the bathroom mirror wiping her bloody nose and busted lip from the punches she received from her own mother. She didn't care where she had to go but she knew for a fact she had to move out her parents' home. Laturi didn't know Christ at that time, but he still blessed her. She stayed with one of her friends who helped her get her grades up, applied for a few scholarships. After graduating high school Laturi moved away and only came home to visit. It has only been about two years since she started talking to her parents.

Laturi was angry at her father for still staying with her mother knowing when she gets too drunk, she gets abusive. "I can't help it Tour-Rie I love her," he would always say. "I believe she's going to change one day."

But the change has never come.

"Hey Tour-Rie, are you okay?" Sha'Bron said caressing her arm.

"Yeah, I'm good I was just thinking about something," Laturi said.

"I like your room it's very nice," Sha'Bron said.

"Thank you," she said with a smile.

"Are you sure you're, okay?" Sha'Bron quizzed.

"Yes, I'm fine," Laturi replied.

"Tour-Rie, you can talk to me about anything," Sha'Bron reassured her.

"I know, do you wanna start going over our wedding plans?" Laturi asked him to try to change the subject.

Before Sha'Bron could say anything Laturi's mother burst into the room. "What are y'all in here doing?" Nadia could barely stand up. Her hair was nappy and in a mess.

Laturi looked into her mother's eyes pleading with her not to embarrass her in front of Sha'Bron.

"Dang how do y'all call yourselves a couple. And don't even touch one another?" Laturi's mother questioned.

"I don't believe in hugging and kissing before marriage," Sha'Bron answered.

"That's a bunch of bullshit you know what I think? I think your gay," Laturi's mother slurred, eyeballing Sha'Bron.

"Momma, stop!" Laturi shrieked.

"Tour-Rie, she's fine she has a right to her opinion. I am not gay I'm saved, and I want to live a life pleasing to Christ," Sha'Bron implied.

Laturi's mother throws her head back and began cackling. "That is the biggest excuse I've ever heard in my life."

"That's the final straw Momma, you are never going to change I'm done trying with you. Come on Bron!" Laturi said. Laturi hastily grabbed a few of her things.

"Where are you going to go? Mistah holy roller ain't gone let you stay at his house," Laturi's mother said.

"I'm going back to stay with Adela and her parents. You have embarrassed me for the last time," Laturi cried.

"Tour-Rie, I don't think your mother means it the way you took it," Sha'Bron tried to explain to her.

"Bron you don't know half the story dealing with my mom. I'm sorry but I've had enough!"

Laturi grabbed her bags and walked them to her car. Sha'Bron didn't say a word he just walked out the door behind Laturi.

~THIRTY-FOUR~

Nadia James was still trying to process what had just happened with her only child Laturi. "I know I haven't been the perfect mother, but I haven't been the worst either. Why does she get so angry at me for being myself?" Nadia said aloud.

"Honey bun, who are you talking to?" Her husband Vincent asked when he walked in.

"I was talking to myself," Nadia said.

"Where is Buttercup?" He asked referring to his pride and joy Laturi.

"She got mad at me again and left with her lil fiancé."

"What did you say this time?" Vincent queried.

"Why does it always have to be me?" Nadia asked glaring at Vincent.

"When you get drunk you don't know what to say and what not to say," Vincent replied.

"Yes, I do I have the freedom of speech don't I?"

"Yeah, ya do but you tend to say things that need to be kept secret. Do you remember all the times you used to get drunk and hurt Buttercup?" Vincent asked.

"Vince I never intended to hurt my own child," Nadia said.

"No, you didn't but when you drink you can't hold yourself to violence and if my baby girl has left again due to your actions this time, I'm not going to be a fool and stay too," Vincent said before storming off down the hallway.

Nadia put her right hand over her forehead. "Is my drinking that bad that I'm causing my husband and only child not to wanna be around me?" Nadia asked herself.

She sat and thought for a moment and remembered at the marriage proposal dinner Shanti saying something about playing devil's advocate with yourself to get to the root of your problems.

"I am not a Christian woman either have I confessed to be, but I don't wanna lose my husband or my daughter because of my own stupidity. If there is a God up there, please help me." Nadia said tears forming in her eyes.

"What made me start drinking like this in the first place?" She asked herself.

Instantly a thought came to Nadia's mind. When she was seven years old her mother abandoned her for some man. Nadia was forced to live with her grandparents who finished raising her. Her grandfather died when she was sixteen. Nadia started drinking to fit in with her peers, but she enjoyed the habit so much it consumed her and took over her life.

Another thought came to her mind when she was sixteen one of her male classmates molested her in the locker room after school other than telling her grandmother or one of the staff members she went home and drank until she passed out on her bed.

There was a bottle of alcohol sitting in front of her she grabbed it and threw it up against the wall the bottle busted and liquor went everywhere.

"I am no longer going to allow this to control my life."

Vincent ran into the living room to see what was going on. "Vince Baby I'm taking control of my life if that's the last thing I do. I don't wanna be this person anymore," Nadia cried.

Vincent grabbed her and held her in his arms. "You got this Honey bun."

~THIRTY-FIVE~

When Trivia opened her eyes, she was lying in a queen-sized bed. All she was wearing was a long t-shirt and boxer shorts. Her throat was swollen and sore.

"Hey babe, about time you woke up," Jett said smiling at her.

"Where am I?" she asked.

"I got us a hotel out of town just in case Lauryn send the cops after me," Jett replied.

"You are still going to be caught," Trivia stated.

Jett didn't utter a word just stared into Trivia's eyes.

Why had it come to this? Jett was not the man he portrayed to be…

Trivia's mind wondered back to a few months before her mother died. Trivia remembered it like it was just yesterday. Her mother was laying in her hospital bed with a red scarf wrapped around her head due to the fact she had lost all of her hair. She was no bigger than a stick.

"Mama what am I going to do without you?" Trivia asked.

"Live your life to the fullest," her mother told her.

"How is that possible I'm only fifteen years old," Trivia cried.

"You will find your way you have all the tools you need." She said referring to her body and good looks.

Trivia's mother dead early one Monday right after Trivia left for school. After her mother died all of her family members refused to take her into their homes but Mickie and her mother took her into theirs, and Mickie treated her like a little sister.

How could I have been so cruel to her? I hope and pray she's not dead so that I can make this up to her. Trivia thought to herself looking over at Jett.

"What are you thinking about baby?" he asked.

"Jett, I have allowed sex and money to cloud my mind. Mickie was there for me when nobody else was and I treated her like crap for a dude. That was low and dumb of me," Trivia said.

"What are you talking about?" Jett asked.

"I'm talking about how I slept with her boyfriend behind her back, inside her house or wherever else. I stood there and allowed a man to harm her. I don't even know if she's alive or dead because I allowed you to force me to leave her on a hardwood floor bleeding." Trivia snared.

Trivia started getting goosebumps just thinking about Mickie lying on the floor her face bruised, a gin shot hole between her eyes and blood pouring out her nose, lips, and mouth, panting for air.

"What are you trying to say Trivia?" Jett spat standing to his feet.

"I'm saying I'm done I'm no longer hurting my family and most importantly I'm no longer hurting myself," Trivia proclaimed.

"You dirty little witch! I took diligent care of you. How are you going to just turn on me like that," Jett spat.

"Jett Beverley first thing first money isn't everything. I see that now. And secondly, I'm not turning on you I'm choosing myself," Trivia said.

"Witch I ought to choke you again and this time kill your trifling behind," Jett threatened.

Trivia could tell Jett was getting angry and was ready to hit her. She quickly grabbed her phone and shot off to the bathroom and locked the door behind her. Jett came to the door kicking and screaming trying to bust in on her. Jett took out his revolver and shot into the ceiling.

"Trivia open this door before I blow it open!" he shouted.

With trembling hands Trivia took a deep breath and began dialing 911.

God, please save me from this situation and I vow to never get caught up like this again. Trivia prayed to herself.

"911 what is your emergency?" A kind woman answered using a caring tone.

"Yes, ma'am my..." Trivia paused for a moment she didn't know what to call Jett at this point he wasn't her boyfriend and by the way he was acting now he wasn't her friend either.

"Hello ma'am is you still there?" The lady asked.

"Yes, ma'am my ex is trying to kill me."

"I am going to send someone out in just a moment can you tell me your location?" the lady asked.

"No ma'am all I know is I'm in a hotel," Trivia said.

God, please help me. Save my life give me one more chance.

A moment later a towel fell from the towel rack and the name on the towel read: Laquita's Sleep Inn 630 Jackson Street.

Thank you, God!

"I am at Laquita's Sleep Inn 630 Jackson Avenue room 303," Trivia informed the lady.

"I will send someone your way in just a minute stay on the phone with me until they get there," the lady instructed.

Tears rolled down Trivia's cheeks while she held the phone listening to Jett twisted the doorknob and try and kicked the door again and again with his feet.

How and why did I allow things in my life to come to this? Money and a life of luxury is not everything.

Jett Beverley looked like a different man as the police officers hauled him away. His once brown eyes that used to warm her heart were now dark and cold as ice.

You will never hurt another person! Trivia thought to herself.

~THIRTY-SIX~

Lauryn sat in a cushioned chair at the head of the bed humming old spiritual songs and combing Mickie's hair. Tears were flowing down her cheeks.

Her husband Charles walked into the room. "You got Mickie looking good," he complimented.

"Thank you," Lauryn said with a half-smile.

He walked over to Lauryn and kissed her lips. "Baby, Mickie is going to pull through this. She made it through the first night with God's grace."

"I know Charles, but I still have my doubts. I never shared this information with you or anyone else but when Mama passed away a couple of months back, I lost some of my faith in God," Lauryn said.

Charles rubbed his chin. "I can understand why you felt that way. You wanted him to heal her on this side of heaven. Sometimes what we want as a yes is a no to Jesus, but we must keep the faith through the good and the bad and trust his plan," Charles said.

"I know but it's so hard Charles. I got my baby girl looking at me to be strong for her and I got my sister needing me to be her strength. How can I be there strength when I'm almost to the point I don't believe anymore. It's so hard Charles," Lauryn said beginning to cry.

"You are one of the strongest people I know God is going to bring you out remember troubles don't last always. Weeping may endure for a night, but Joy comes in the morning," Charles informed her.

Lauryn leaned over and gave Charles a kiss on the lips. "I love you so much Charles Laughlin," she said.

"I love you too Lauryn Laughlin."

"Ew get a room," Shanti sarcastically said as she entered the room.

"Hey Baby girl," Charles said, standing to his feet going to hug his daughter.

"Hey Daddy," Shanti said giving him a hug and kiss on the cheek.

"Where's Stephon?" Charles asked.

"He had some things to finish up before work tomorrow," Shanti said.

Shanti walked over to Lauryn and gave her a hug. "How are you holding up?"

"I'm good," Lauryn said giving her daughter a big smile.

Even though Lauryn was smiling on the outside her heart was aching on the inside nobody, but Jesus Christ her Lord and Savior understood her pain.

A few seconds later someone knocked on the door.

"Come in," Charles and Shanti said in unison.

A short petite woman with long wavy red hair that was tied up in a huge bun walked into the room. "Good evening, I'm Lindsey I'm Ms. Pearson's nurse for tonight. Are all of you, her family?" Lindsey asked looking at each one of them.

"Yes, we are," Shanti spoke up.

"Doctor Darwin? Is that you?" Lindsey asked surprised to see Shanti.

"Yes, ma'am it is," Shanti replied.

"I haven't seen you since nursing school, it's so nice seeing you," Lindsey said.

"It's nice to see you as well."

"Now back to Ms. Pearson after running a few tests we found she has minor encephalitis meaning swollen brain tissues caused by the forced trauma to her head, and some hemorrhaging around her brain we are working hard to stop…" was all Lindsey got out before Lauryn stopped her.

"Is she going to be, okay?" Lauryn asked holding her hand over her nose and mouth trying to stop her flow of tears.

"To be honest with you it's hard to tell right now Ms. Pearson still has a long recovery process," Lindsey informed. Charles and Shanti looked over at Lauryn both of them could tell she wasn't taking the news easily. "Lindsey can you please give us a minute and come back later," Shanti asked kindly.

"Sure." Lindsey said walking out pulling the door up behind her.

"Let's join hands and pray God can turn any situation around," Shanti insisted.

"Baby, hold Mickie's hand while we pray," Charles enjoined.

Lauryn squeezed Mickie's hand while Charles prayed a powerful prayer for her healing.

After the prayer ended. There was a loud knock at the door., Shanti walked over to open it.

"Hey Shanti," a familiar voice greeted Shanti.

"Hey Trivia, come in," Shanti said with a smile.

Lauryn glared in Trivia's direction. "You got a lot of nerve coming in this room after all you did to my sister," Lauryn snarled. "Lauryn that's why I came by I'm sorry," Trivia pleaded.

"It's too late to be sorry now you should have thought about that before you hurt her," Lauryn growled.

Who do this chick think she is coming into my sister's hospital room giving a weak behind apology. Lauryn thought to herself. She was infuriated to say the least.

"Lauryn I'm so sorry, please forgive me. I called around to every hospital closed by trying to check and see did Mickie pull through…"

"Why so you can help that low down dirty dawg finish her off!" Lauryn spat.

"It's nothing like that, Jet abused me too, when I went against him for what he did to Mickie." Trivia said pointing to her bruised neck. "I was dumb and stupid please forgive Lauryn," Trivia pleased with Lauryn.

"I'll have to pray about that because you did some messed up crap," Lauryn said.

A tear rolled down Trivia's cheek as she turned and walked out the door.

Charles and Shanti stood in silence until Trivia left.

"What was all that about?" Shanti asked no longer able to hold her silence.

"I don't wanna get into it right now," Lauryn said.

"Forgiveness is important," Charles added.

"I'll forgive when the time is right for me," Lauryn said.

"Baby, you can't be that way, think about what Jesus would want from you?" Charles tried making Lauryn remember.

Lord, I know you want us to forgive and forget but how can I forgive someone who helped cause my sister to be laying in a hospital bed fighting for her life.

Lauryn thought to herself. "Charles, I am so tired of people telling me to forgive and forget sometimes you gotta let people know their mistakes have consequences," Lauryn said through gritted teeth.

"I understand where you're coming from Baby. I really do but you know that's not the way Christ wants us to feel or handle things," Charles reminded her.

Lauryn threw her hand up and walked over to Mickie's bedside and begin running her hands through her hair. "I love you so much Sis you have to pull through this," Lauryn whispered in Mickie's ear.

She glanced over at her husband and daughter as they walked out the room.

I know I'm coming off a bit harsh, but I can't just forgive Trivia like that.

~THIRTY-SEVEN~

"Mama, can I talk to you outside really quick?" Shanti asked giving her mother Lauryn a serious look.

"I don't wanna leave Mickie's side," Lauryn said without giving Shanti eye contact.

"Mama, come outside please," Shanti demanded.

Finally, Lauryn looked into Shanti's eyes and seen that she was serious.

"I'll be back Mick," Lauryn whispered in Mickie's ears, before joining Shanti at the door.

"Mama, I have never disrespected you, but Daddy is right you need to forgive Jett and Trivia for what happened to Untee Mickie," Shanti said.

"Shanti, it's easy for you to say you don't understand how I feel right now," Lauryn stated.

"What do you mean by that Mama?" Shanti asked.

Shanti could feel her pressure rising she wanted to scream and shout at her mother so badly.

I don't understand. I don't understand what because I have forgiven people I didn't want to forgive. My Mama can be so stubborn sometimes.

"What I mean is you don't understand anything about how I feel right now Shanti."

Shanti sucked in some air. "Mama I do understand how you feel I have forgiven people who felt didn't deserve it and one of the hardest thing I had to do here recently is forgive myself," Shanti blurted out.

"What do you mean Baby girl?" Lauryn asked.

"Mama, I never said anything to you or Daddy but when Me-Ma passed away I went through depression for almost two months lying in bed crying my eyes not eating or drinking anything. I almost died simply because I blamed myself for Me-Ma dying. I battled myself and I was losing that battle. I even stopped praying and talking to Jesus. It wasn't until I forgave myself and stop having a pity party that I was able to forgive myself and bounce back. I said all that to say Mama forgiveness is particularly important and if you don't forgive someone it will consume you and take over you."

Lauryn stood quiet for a moment before uttering a sound... "Shanti, why didn't you let me, and your father know something was going on with you. I woke up many nights praying and crying for you and Mickie, but I didn't understand why... Now I do you were going through depression and Mick was going through things with Jet from now on don't keep your father and I out of your life Shanti," Lauryn scolded her.

"I want Mama, I'm okay now Sty and the kids were there for me but most importantly I had to be there for myself. Mama that is why you need to forgive," Shanti said.

Lauryn takes a deep breath. "Will you pray with me?"

"Absolutely," Shanti smiled.

Lauryn turned to face Shanti and stretched out her arms so did Shanti they grabbed each other's hands and begin praying and crying out to God for Lauryn's healing and forgiveness for herself and for Jet and Trivia.

After the prayer was over Lauryn began crying and hugging her daughter.

"I am so blessed to have you as my daughter," Lauryn said through her tears.

"I am blessed to have you as my mom," Shanti said.

Charles ran out into the hallway grasping for breath. "I just paged the nurse something is going on with Mickie she started moaning and groaning and then her monitor went off," he shrieked.

Shanti could see and feel her father's fear and she too was in fear.

God we can't take another loss not right now.

Shanti held her mother in her arms while she sobbed.

Everything looked as though it was moving in slow motion the doctors and nurses running in and out of the room trying to get Mickie stabled.

"We are losing her!" one of the doctors yelled.
God please not another loss please Father God Lord Jesus

~THIRTY-EIGHT~

Laturi sat quietly at the table barely touching her food.
"Are you okay?" Sha'Bron asked.
"Yeah I'm good," Laturi answered barely looking from the floor.

Laturi hated lying to her future husband, but she was not ready to confine in him about her problems with her mother. Ever since she walked out her parents' house days ago she has been feeling bad for her mother. *Why was her mother an alcoholic?*

"Tour-Rie, I been around you long enough to know when something is bothering you," Sha'Bron said.

Before Laturi could answer him her parents walked to their table.

"Tour-Rie, I know I'm probably the last person you wanna hear from, but I need to talk to you, and I need you to hear me out," Nadia said.

"Mama, I'm not in the mood for one of your fake apologies," Laturi said.

"Tour-Rie please here me okay," Nadia pleaded.

"Tour-Rie, listen to what she has to say if you two need privacy I'll go to a different table," Sha'Bron suggested.

"I haven't had anything to drink in two days since you walked out the door. I need your help Tour-Rie," Nadia said trying to fight back her tears.

"Is this true Daddy?" Laturi asked looking up at her father.

"Yes it is Buttercup, your mother is trying to change," Vincent chimed in.

Laturi popped up from her seat and pulled her mother into a hug. "I am so proud of Mama!"

"Thank you Tour-Rie," Nadia said wiping fallen tears from her eyes.

"Have a seat," Laturi said.

Nadia pulled a chair up beside Laturi and put her hand on her knee. "I have kept a lot of things about my past from you and your father but the only thing keeping it has done is destroyed my life… I am sorry I was never the mother you needed me to be because I was too busy fighting my own personal battles. One night when I was only seven years old my mother stayed out all night with one of her male friends she didn't leave me much food or anything I basically had to fend for myself. My mother came home just before daybreak the next morning and told me to pack my clothes I'm going to live with my grandparents because she was tired of me messing up her life causing men to walk out on her. So, she dropped me off at her parents' house and for weeks and even months I cried for my mother begging for answers on why she no longer wanted me. I didn't see my mother again until I was over thirty years old. I tried so hard to be a better woman than her, but I failed you tremendously and I'm so sorry," Nadia cried.

"Mama, I'm so sorry I never knew," Laturi said running her hand up and down her mother's back.

"Neither did I why you never told me about this?" Vincent asked putting his arms around his wife's waist.

"I was too ashamed to tell anyone and there's more to my story…" Nadia began and paused.

"Let it all out Mama so Christ can heal and deliver you," Laturi added.

"This is the hardest part of my life to open up about when I was sixteen my grandfather passed away in August and later in that same month a couple of my so-called friend guys from school lied and told me they had brought a gift to offer their condolences. They got me in the locker room and molested me, my grandmother had so much going trying to adjust to losing my grandfather that I didn't wanna bother her with that nonsense I walked home went into her liquor cabinet and started drinking and I never stopped. I started drinking so much that it took over my life I felt like I had to have alcohol to function."

"I am so sorry you went through that," Sha'Bron spoke up. "Let's join hands and pray."

Laturi placed her hand in her mother's hand and her father did the same while Sha'Bron put on hand in Laturi's other hand and his other hand on Nadia's head.

"Father God Lord Jesus, I come to you now humbly as I know how asking you to heal, deliver, and set Ms. Nadia free from her alcoholic addiction and the past that has haunted her for years let her know that in you Lord she has the victory. In Jesus name I pray Amen."

"Amen," everyone said in unison.

"Thank you so much Bron. I am so glad Tour-Rie found a good man like you," Nadia said reaching her arms out to give Sha'Bron a hug.

"Thank you," Sha'Bron said.

I feel so bad talking to my mother like I have all these years and treating her like she was nothing when she has been through so much in her life. Laturi thought to herself.

"What's on your mind Tour-Rie?" Sha'Bron asked.

"I feel so bad about how I treated you over the years you don't deserve it Mama you have been through so much already," Laturi said.

"It's okay baby. If you wanna help me, introduce me to Christ and help me get a relationship with him," Nadia said.

"Come to my grandfather's church on Sunday," Sha'Bron offered.

"I would love it…Your father and I have an engagement to get to I just wanted to stop by and try to make things right between us," Nadia said.

"I love you guys," Laturi said hugging her parents and seeing them out the restaurant.

"I hope that Christ heals your mother and set her soul free," Sha'Bron said.

"Me too."

~THIRTY-NINE~

Kendal sat at Mickie's bedside praying and crying out to God to heal her and not take her away from him or her family.

How could God allow him to have these feelings for her and try and take her away before he could tell her how much he really loved her and cared about her. It wasn't far by a long shot in his eyes.

We have too many more memories to share Kendal thought to himself while he gazed upon her beautiful face some of the bruising had gone down and her natural beauty shined through like the sun. It was something about a woman's natural beauty that Kendal loved the most he was never a man who looked makeup, false hair, eyebrows, and eyelashes everything naturally. That was one of the things he loved so much about Mickie she was simply just beautiful.

While he was deep in thought he heard her moan.

"Mickie, it's me Kendal I am here with you, you are not alone baby," he leaned over and whispered in her ear.

Mickie began to move her head and neck from side to side letting out an even louder moan. Her eyes began batting like she was trying to open them.

Kendal's heart began beating faster.

"Jesus could it be! Could Mickie finally be waking up?" Kendal said to himself.

Kendal squeezes Mickie's hand tightly but not tight enough to hurt her. "C'mon Mickie. I love you please come back to me," he pleaded.

Mickie eyes began batting again this time even more forcefully and faster as though she was fighting to open them her hands and feet began to move next.

Kendal stared with astonishment as Mickie fought to open her eyes and move her body.

Mickie's eyes opened and she glanced over at Kendal.

"Thank You Jesus!" he bellowed.

Squeezing her hand and staring into her hands trying to cry he said. "I love you Mickie I am so happy to see those beautiful eyes again."

Kendal stood up to page the nurse to let them know Mickie had opened her eyes, but Mickie began moaning when he moved. "Don't worry Baby I'm not going to leave your side."

After calling for the nurse to come in and check her Kendal sat with Mickie and held her hand.

"Mickie I promise to never allow another person to harm you. I am so sorry I didn't fight harder that day to keep you at work. I can be a bit stubborn sometimes," Kendal said.

Mickie nodded her head in agreement as a single tear rolled down her cheek.

I wish I knew what she's thinking or feeling at this moment. Kendal thought to himself.

Kayla walked into the room after greeting Kendal. She went about her business checking to see if everything was okay with Mickie. "Sir, can you please step out for a moment?" she asked.

"Sure," Kendal said.

Kendal let go of Mickie's hand and turned to walk out the door.

"Ken-Ken...dal don't leave me," Mickie forced herself to say.

Kendal turned around and said. "I will never leave you Baby never again."

He pasted back and forth up and down the hallway waiting for the nurse to come and let him know how Mickie was doing. While he was waiting he called Lauryn to let her know Mickie had opened her eyes.

By the time Kayla allowed Kendal back into the room Lauryn and Charles were there as well. Kayla greeted them.

"Is she going to be okay?" Lauryn and Kendal asked at the same time.

"Yes she is, She made a speedy recovery the only thing is… due to the trauma her body faced it is going to be a lengthy process for her to gain her feeling back in her legs meaning she going to need therapy to help her walk again and some thoughts that may come natural to the human mind are not going to be able to come as quickly to her. With a lot of time, therapy, and patience she will soon be where she needs to be," Kayla said with a smile.

Lauryn rushed into the room to hug and kiss her sister.

"Hey Mick, I love you so much girl," Lauryn gushed.

"I-I love you," Mickie stammered.

"Hey darling you, you gave a scare," Charles said giving her a hug.

"Me too," Mickie said.

"Do you remember anything from that night?" Lauryn asked.

"More than I care to," Mickie said. "All I remember after laying on that cold floor is me praying begging God for another chance not to let me die," Mickie said as tears began spilling down her face. "Who found me?"

"I did, and I wish I would have made it to you sooner," Kendal uttered.

"It's not your fault," Mickie said.

"I wish I would have fight harder because seeing you like that really broke my heart and I made a promise to God, you and myself that when he brought you through I would never allow anyone or anything else harm you."

"Thank you," Mickie said.

"I love you Mickie I mean that," Kendal said.

Lauryn and Charles stood side by side looking at Kendal and Mickie talking to one another.

"They remind you of a younger version of us don't they?" Charles asked Lauryn.

"What you mean by younger you are still the love of my life, and I know for a fact I am yours," Lauryn said.

"And you are right Laurie bug," Charles said before giving Lauryn a kiss on her lips.

"You see how your sister and brother-in-law are that's how I wanna love you and make you feel Mickie. No more drama and No more Pain," Kendal promised Mickie.

~FORTY~

Sitting on the edge of the hospital bed Mickie sat patiently and quietly waiting for her older sister Lauryn and her husband Charles to take her to their home to help take care of her until she was able to take care of herself again.

As she sat in the room alone, she tried so desperately not to think of that awful night, but it seemed no matter how hard she tried to forget her mind would still drift back and thoughts would resurface causing an onslaught of pain, hurt, anger and sadness that she was trying to overcome.

Mickie had been a good woman to Jett Beverley not perfect but good as could be. How could he treat her like she was the scum of the earth?

How could someone go from worshipping the grounds you walked on to hating your guts, almost taking your life, and leaving you for dead? Mickie thought to herself.

An image from that ghastly night played in her mind. Jett was standing over her with a look of hate and disgust he was not the man she had once shared so many lovely memories with. The silver baseball bat came down hard on her flesh as he drew back with all his might.

A single tear rolled down her cheek as the memory played in her mind.

"I refuse to cry I am going to recover from this and move on with my life. Besides, I have a whole future ahead of me," Mickie said to herself.

"Knock…knock," Lauryn announced slightly pushing the door

open.

"Hey sis, I'm in here," Mickie said giving Lauryn a smile.

"Are you ready to get this show on the road?" Lauryn asked.

"Yes, I am. I have out stayed my welcome in this place," Mickie chuckled.

"Before we leave and before Charles comes in, I would like to discuss something with you," Lauryn said sitting down beside Mickie.

I am a little too old for rules sis and I can't do too much movement so what is there to tell me? Mickie thought to herself.

"What's up?" Mickie asked.

"I want you to know that I love you more than you could ever imagine. I know I haven't been the best sister in the world and there for you like I should have but I promise to never fail you like that again. Temetria I don't know what I would have done if you would have died," Lauryn said.

Mickie placed her hand in Lauryn's hand. "Lauryn communication is a two-way street I was too busy chasing after a man who didn't want me or care for me at all. I lost focus on the important things in life, and I lost focus of myself. We both could have made better decisions when it came to our relationship, but we are here now and that's all that matters," Mickie said with a smile.

"You are so right. I love you Temetria," Lauryn said leaning over to give Mickie a hug.

"I love you too…stop calling me by my government name," Mickie scolded her playfully.

"Hey, are you ladies ready to go?" Charles quizzed stepping into the room.

"I'm just waiting on my nurse to bring my discharge paperwork," Mickie informed.

Momentarily nurse Kayla walked into the room with a bright smile and a clipboard. "Are you guys waiting for me?" She jovial.

"Yes, ma'am we are," Mickie chuckled.

"Now that I got my joke out the way let's get down to busy, Ms. Pearson you are signed up for three therapy sessions a week to help with learning how to walk and move your body again you don't have any food restrictions, but I do ask you to please take good care of yourself," Kayla said giving Mickie a hug.

"Thank you I will," Mickie said.

Kayla greets Lauryn and Charles before excusing herself.

"Alrighty then let's get this show on the road," Charles said walking to the bed to lift Mickie into her wheelchair.

"I'll get her," Kendal announced.

Charles and Lauryn smiled and stepped back to give Kendal some room.

Kendal walked over to the bedside and gave Mickie a hug and kiss on the forehead. "I meant everything I said to you. I want to love you, protect you and stand by your side," Kendal soothed her.

"Thank you," Mickie said softly.

"Put your arms around my neck," Kendal told her.

"Kendal, I'm heavy and dead weight I don't want to hurt you."

"That is a bunch of none-sense put your arms around my neck."

After trying to protest and lost Mickie put her arms around Kendal's neck and laid her head on his shoulder.

It felt so good being in someone's arms who genuinely cared for her.

Kendal spend her around a couple times before putting her in her wheelchair causing her to laugh while Lauryn and Charles clapped their hands.

I am beginning to think that after all my dark days the sun is finally shining on me.

~FORTY-ONE~

The bell rang for the students' fifteen-minutes break and within minutes, students erupted from their classrooms filling the hallways with laughter, loud chatter, and small shoves as they worked feverishly to join their respective cliques.

Harmony Darwin and her two best friends Kiana Morgan and Brenley Johnson met at their favorite bench beside the stone-carved tiger mascot and without hesitation begin discussing the hottest topic of the day homecoming.

Bursting open her bag of potato chips Kiana was the first to speak up. "Harmony, I am so proud of you!" Have you picked out your dress yet?"

"My Mom and I are going after school today," Harmony replied with a smile.

"I can't wait to see your dress. I know you are going to be beautiful," Brenley chimed in.

"I hope so," Harmony said.

"Girl, Ms. Shanti has great taste and wasn't she the first African American homecoming queen at Bale High her senior year?" Kiana asked.

"Yes and she was the first African American valedictorian," Harmony said.

"Wow," the girls said in unison.

"I remember my Mom telling me her sophomore year of high school is when she first started talking to my Dad," Harmony said.

"Your parents been together that long.," Kiana gushed.

"Yes," Harmony said.

"On another note, Harmony, Kiana and I were wondering are you attending the homecoming dance this year?" Brenley asked.

"Of course, I am but I don't have a date yet," Harmony responded.

"Who do you want to take?" the girls quizzed in unison.

Harmony smiles shyly, "I kind of want to ask Galen Milliner."

The two girls looked at each other in disbelief. Galen was notorious around the campus for sleeping around with a lot of girls.

"Umm… Harmony are you okay?" Brenley asked.

"She must have lost her mind! Do you know what kind of guy Galen is? Your brother would kill you and him!" Kiana snared.

Harmony shrugged her shoulders. "Yeah I know but I think he's cute," she whispered looking intensely across the yard at him high-five one of the other football players.

Galen you can't be that bad.

The bell rang interrupting their break.

"Harmony I'm not being mean I just don't want to see you get hurt," Kiana replied.

"I know," Harmony said.

The student filled the hallways again rushing to their next class when one of the football player's ran into Harmony knocking her book out her arms.

"Excuse me I'm sorry," he said when turned around to help her grab her book and notebook off the floor.

"It's okay," Harmony replied without making eye contact.

"You're Harmony Darwin right?" he asked.

"Yes how do you know?"

"Maybe if you made eye contact with me you would know who I am," he said.

Slowly Harmony held her head up and gasped when she looked into the eyes of her crush Galen Milliner.

Galen smiled.

Harmony's heart skipped a beat as a flattering feeling hit her stomach.

"Hey Galen," she said once she collected herself and her thoughts.

"Hey Harmony, would you like me to walk to class?" he asked.

"Sure."

"Are you going to the homecoming dance?" Galen asked.

"I want to, but I don't have a date," Harmony said.

"Well, it's your lucky day neither do I," Galen laughed. "Would you like to go with me?"

Harmony could not believe her ears Galen Milliner asked her to the homecoming dance.

"I would love to," Harmony purred.

"Great I'll see you after the carnation," Galen said running down the hall.

Now the only problem is getting my parents and my two older brothers to be okay with the idea.

~FORTY-TWO~

A burst of wind swept through the air, causing the trees to dance and show off their beautiful fall colors. A sea of orange, red, and mustard leaves slowly danced away from their lifeline and fell to their death.

It was the Friday of Homecoming for Bale, Alabama. Shanti glanced at the scenery while her husband drove by admiring all the small businesses already prepared for the festivities. Outside of their annual Fall festival, Homecoming had always been one of the main events to bring their community together.

For a brief moment Shanti thought back on how fun it used to be for her when she was a student at Bale City Schools during this majestic week; dressing up in different themes during the week, helping decorate the floats, decorating the classroom doors and hallways was only half of the fun. She looked over her shoulder at her oldest daughter sitting in the backseat dressed like the queen she was a smile gradually took over her face.

I really wish Me-Ma were here to witness how beautiful Harmony is today.

"What's on your mind? Baby," Stephon asked.

"Some of everything, do you remember how much fun we used to have during homecoming week?" Shanti asked with a huge smile.

"Yes ma'am I do. It used to be so magical," Stephon said. "But my favorite homecoming was homecoming of 97'."

"Why is that?" Shanti asked giving a seductive look.

"I received a letter from the prettiest fifteen-year-old girl in the world asking me to be her date to the homecoming dance," Stephon smiled enticingly.

Shanti giggled and squeezed Stephon's free hand. "I love you Stephon Darwin."

"I love you Shanti Darwin."

"Mama… Daddy, I have a quick question to ask?" Harmony asked.

"What is it darling?" Stephon asked using a drawl causing everyone in the car to laugh.

"There's this boy at school named Galen Milliner he asked me to the homecoming dance can I please go?" Harmony pleaded.

"Are you talking about the Galen that your brother said pry on naïve girls?" Stephon asked.

"Yes, sir that's the one," Harmony said.

"I don't think that's a good idea Harmony," Stephon said.

"But Daddy!" Harmony whined.

"No buts Harmony the answer is no," Stephon said.

Shanti sat quietly for a moment and thought back on when she was fifteen and first made it known to her family and friends. She liked Stephon her parents acted the same way towards her. This Galen kid could be just like Stephon people making up stories on him and having opinions about him without knowing him.

"Stephon, how about we get her to bring Galen by the house an hour before the dance so that we can meet him and then we decide if she should go with him or not," Shanti insisted.

"My answer is no and I'm sticking with that," Stephan replied firmly.

"Do you remember a sixteen-year-old boy and a fifteen-year-old girl that was faced with that same issue people judging but that girl fought to change people's opinion of that boy, and her parents were the same way," Shanti recalled.

Letting out a deep sigh. "Yes, I remember it's not right to place judgement too quickly. Harmony just do as your mother said and bring him by the house and we will go from there."

"Thank you, guys," Harmony gushed.

When they arrived at the school Stephon got out first, he opened the door to help Harmony out the back and together they walked to the passenger side, and he opened the door for Shanti.

"You both look amazing," Shanti said looking at Harmony dressed in her long lavender mermaid style gown.

My baby is not a baby anymore she's all grown up. Shanti thought to herself as a single tear fell from her eyes. She looked at Stephon and knew he was thinking the same thing. "Baby, how about you go ahead and start heading to the football field so I can have a quick talk with Harmony," Shanti instructed.

Stephon nodded his head leaving the ladies to talk.

"Sweet Pea you look stunning," Shanti said with adoration in her eyes.

"Thanks Mama," Harmony replied.

Terricka the sophomore attendant walked up to Harmony and Shanti. Terricka was five feet and eight inches tall, with a warm espresso complexion, long mink eyelashes, her hair was in a top knot bun with a bang.

"Hello Ms. Darwin and Hello Harmony, your dress is cute, but you look like a plain Jane nothing about you sticks out," Terricka replied.

Hold your peace and let the Lord fight your battles.

Lord I'm trying to be the bigger person, but that little girl is asking for with all that make-up on her face she could start her own clown service.

Be kind.

I'm trying.

"Young lady I think it is time for you to go find your family," Shanti said with a forceful smile.

"Yes ma'am, see you on the field Harmony," Terricka said hurrying off.

"Harmony don't allow what that girl said bother you," Shanti said.

"Mama she's right I am just a plain Jane I'm not beautiful like the rest of the girls in my class and you make me wear skirts and dresses all the time. It's getting old," Harmony whined.

"Harmony, I know what you are going through I was a young teenage girl growing up once myself. I'm going to tell you a story about myself when I was your age my mother found out I wore a pair of tight-fitting jeans, low-cut blouse and make-up to school trying to impress a guy. My mama was infuriated when she picked me up from school. We bickered all the way from the school to Me-Ma's and then we continued when we walked through the door. Me-Ma intervened and ask my mama could she talk to me, and mama allowed her to. Me-Ma gave that you know you're wrong look. I dropped my head because I hated to disappoint her. Me-Ma quietly asked me Shani girl do you know where diamonds come from? I told her no. Me-Ma told me diamonds are located deep under earth's surface under all the dirt and crust but a diamond shines bright there are replicas out there which are rhinestones man-made diamonds that you can get anywhere. A diamond is covered up waiting on the right miner to find them and appreciate their value. Harmony you are a diamond and that's how you should carry yourself no matter what," Shanti explained.

"Thank you, Mama, I needed to hear that," Harmony said giving Shanti a hug.

"You are welcome now go make your mama proud," Shanti smiled.

~FORTY-THREE~

Mickie sat quietly on Kendal's loveseat sofa holding her bible, pen, and notebook in her lap. Her body was attentive, but her mind was elsewhere.

Lord, I know I shouldn't be thinking about my ex-boyfriend, but I can't seem to get him off my mind. Mickie thought to herself.

Kendal sat beside her in an armchair. Lauryn and Charles sat across from them on the long sofa Lauryn at one end and Charles on the other.

I hope to one day have a love and marriage like theirs but if I can't shake my feelings for Jett I can kiss that goodbye.

"Kendal I wanna thank you for allowing Lauryn and me into your home," Charles said.

"You are more than welcome Pastor Laughlin," Kendal replied with a smile.

Mickie listened the best she could to the small talk Lauryn, Kendal, and Charles were having. She didn't want to seem to distant, but her mind was scattered into a million separate places. Kendal glanced in her direction for a brief moment. "Is everything okay Mickie?" He asked finally.

"Yes," Mickie answered quickly.

"Mickie, are you sure you answered that pretty fast," Lauryn chimed in.

Mickie held her head up and looked from Lauryn to Kendal briefly. "Yes, I'm sure."

Kendal had known Mickie long enough to know when something

was bothering her, and this time was no different but to get it out of her was the part he hadn't mastered yet.

Kendal moved closer to Mickie. "Baby, I want you to know you can tell me anything," Kendal held her hand in his hand.

Mickie takes a deep breath and gives Kendal a sincere look. "Kendal please don't try to talk me out of this because I need this to help move on..." Mickie begin and paused.

"What is it?" Kendal asked.

"I wanna go to the county jail to visit Jett.," Mickie blurted out.

"That's why you kept asking me where he was yesterday," Kendal said. He turned his body so that he was looking directly into her eyes.

"Yes, but I need closure from that relationship," Mickie added.

"Mickie, he beat you, left you for dead, he treated you like garbage and cheated on you with your own flesh and blood right in front of your face. What closure could you possibly need from that scrum bag?" Lauryn hissed.

"Laurie, you don't understand," Mickie said.

"No, I don't, and I'm neither do I want to. Let the past be the past and move on Mickie," Lauryn demanded.

"Laurie, I respect your opinion, but this is for me not you," Mickie retorted. Mickie could feel her pressure rising.

Lauryn have always tried to force her thoughts and beliefs on Mickie, but one thing Lauryn forgot Mickie is here own person with her own thoughts and beliefs.

Kendal could tell the heat was rising between the two sisters. "Mickie, I see this is important to you allow me to drive you there so that I can be with you," Kendal insisted.

After a moment of hesitation Mickie finally agreed.

"Mickie please be careful, and Kendal please take care of her," Lauryn said.

"Laurie he's going to be behind a glass he can't do anything to harm me," Mickie said.

"I promise to keep her safe," Kendal said.

Charles prayed over Mickie and Kendal before they departed.

~FORTY-FOUR~

Trivia sat anxiously waiting for her best friend Sophie to arrive at her apartment.

"This cannot be happening to me, Lord please don't let it be what I think it is," Trivia said aloud as she ran her hands through hair tangled hair.

The doorbell rang.

"Come on in," Trivia shouted from her comfortable spot on her sofa.

"Hey bookie, what's up?" Sophie sang.

Sophie ran to Trivia threw her arms around her waist and pulled her into a hug. Trivia laid her head on Sophie's shoulder.

"Sophie, I am so scared," Trivia stated.

"There is nothing to be scared of. What are your symptoms?" Sophie quizzed.

The two ladies ended their embrace and sat side by side facing one another.

"Where do I begin…first thing I can barely get a good night sleep due to the fact I'm up all night using the bathroom, I can't even touch or bump my nipples because they're so tender, my breast are getting bigger none of my bras fit anymore, I can walk from my bedroom to the kitchen and I am already out of breath, and last but not least I'm always wanting to cry like right now…" Trivia started crying hysterically.

Sophie put her arms around Trivia held her in her arms. "You are going to be okay?" she whispered in Trivia's ear.

"What do I do now?" Trivia cried looking up at her best friend for answers.

"We are going to the store to buy you a pregnancy test," Sophie announced.

"I can't be pregnant not right now," Trivia cried.

"Trivia get yourself together you are going to be okay. I am here for you," Sophie said.

"I know but I am so scared right now. I can't be pregnant with Jet's baby," Trivia cried.

Trivia slumped over and began crying hysterically. "I really messed up this time."

"Let me enlighten you on something when I first found out I was having my twins Carlee and Caylen I was devastated because the last thing I wanted to do was have baby by Caleb, but my two babies are a blessing from God and I wouldn't trade them for anything in the world," Sophie encouraged Trivia.

Trivia's mouth dropped and she let out a gasp the moment she looked down at her pregnancy test.

Jesus this cannot be happening to me I cannot be carrying Jett Beverley's baby. She said to herself. Her body been to shake involuntarily as tears began to fall down her cheeks.

"Jesus why me?" Trivia cried.

Sophie ran into the bathroom and intuitively knew what was wrong with her dear friend.

"It's going to be okay Trivia," Sophie promised her.

"What do I do now?" Trivia asked.

"Do you wanna tell him about the baby?" Sophie asked. "It's your decision."

"Yes, I'm not going to be that cruel," Trivia said.

"Okay and after that we are going to make you a doctor's appointment so that you can find out how far along you are," Sophie said.

Trivia nodded her head in agreement.

~FOURTY-FIVE~

The faded baby blue roof was the first scenery Mickie noticed as Kendal drove into the county jail's visitor parking lot. The spiked metal fence warning all inmates to stay inside their doomed prison was the next thing she noticed.

How could anyone willingly end up in a place like this? Mickie asked herself.

"Are you okay?" Kendal asked interrupting her thoughts.

"Yes, I'm fine," Mickie sighed.

What is this visit with Jett going to be like? I haven't seen him since the night he tried to take my life. Mickie thought to herself.

"Are you having second thoughts?" Kendal asked.

"No, not really… I just have a strange uneasy feeling," Mickie replied.

"Do you wanna head back home?" Kendal questioned her.

"No Kendal I'm doing this okay," Mickie huffed.

Raising his hand in total surrender Kendal said. "My bad ma'am I'll be quiet."

"I didn't mean it to come out like that," Mickie said.

"It's all good."

Kendal found a parking place and pulled in. He turned off the ignition and turned towards Mickie… "You ready to go in?" Kendal asked.

"Yes, I am and thank you for being so supportive," Mickie said.

Kendal stepped out the car and walked over to the passenger side to help Mickie out. Mickie had come along way with her rehabilitation, but she still had a way to go. Mickie could now walk on her own with the help of a boot on her left foot. Slowly and gently, Kendal helped her ease her left leg out the door making sure not to bump the boot against the door or get it hung on the door.

"Alrighty your all set let's go do this," Kendal replied.

"Kendal, I want to go back there alone if you don't mind," Mickie pleaded.

"Why?" Kendal questioned her without thinking twice.

"I want Jet to show me the real him if he knows you are there, he will be a coward and back down," Mickie said.

"I hope you know what you are doing Mickie," Kendal replied.

Mickie stands on her tippy-toes and kisses Kendal's cheek. "I do and I'll be okay."

Mickie and Kendal walked slowly to the entrance. Kendal hurried in front of Mickie so that he could open the door for her.

There was a small, crowded room with two rows of metal chairs. The room was small, dark, and gloomily.

"Can I help you?" a short plump older woman with a milk chocolate complexion with salt and pepper box braids asked looking up at Mickie.

"Yes ma'am, I am here to see Jett Beverley," Mickie said.

"You are the second visit in line for him," the lady replied.

Who else could be here visiting Jett? Mickie asked in her mind but refused to ask aloud. And besides, it did not matter she was there to clear her mind free of him.

"Ma'am did you hear me?" the lady asked.

"Oh, I'm sorry I must have zoned out for a moment," Mickie said.

"May I see your license?" the lady asked.

Mickie reached inside her purse and handed the lady her license out of her wallet.

After scanning over Mickie's identification card for a moment and typing something on the computer she handed Mickie back her card. "Have a seat you will be able to see him in just a second."

"Is everything good?" Kendal asked once Mickie was seated next to him.

"Yeah," Mickie said with a smile.

"Okay ladies you may head in the back now," the lady announced.

While they were walking in the back to visit the inmates someone bumped Mickie's shoulder.

"Excuse me I'm sorry," a woman said.

The voice sounded familiar to Mickie but without being able to see her face Mickie could not make out who the lady was. Mickie walked in front of the lady and realized who she was…The lady gasped when she seen it was Mickie and Mickie could feel her pressure rising.

"Trivia!" Mickie shouted causing everyone to stop and stare at them.

"Hey Mickie, this visit is not what you think it is," Trivia stammered.

"Save it Trivia! Save it! You know what? Ever since I found out you were sleeping with my man behind my back, I never confronted you or said anything to you…"

"Mickie this is not the time or place for this," Trivia whispered scanning the area of all the faces turned around staring at them.

"When and where is the time, Trivia? You were wrong and you know you was wrong," Mickie lowered her voice trying not to cause a scene.

"I don't know Mickie.," Trivia lowered her head.

"Oh, don't act ashamed now… you were not ashamed when you were laying up with him in the house we shared, taking the money that he should have been putting in our house. You know the part that hurts the most is that I love you like a little sister and treated you like the little sister I never had and then you betray me like this, but then again how can you expect a tramp to be loyal to anyone," Mickie replied.

"Hold on wait a minute, Mickie."

"No, you listen to me you are a sick and pathetic individual Trivia going around hurting people who have done nothing but love and care about you," Mickie huffed.

"It's not like that Mickie," Trivia cried.

"Whatever, I should be beating your behind right now, but I refuse to stoop down to your level and act like a piece of trash," Mickie turned up her nose in disgust.

Jett's mouth dropped open the moment he seen Mickie and Trivia standing before him.

"Hey ladies," he muttered.

"Jett, we need to talk," Trivia said.

"Dang, do you have to always be so rude," Mickie asked with an attitude.

"Mickie what I was trying to tell you in the hallway, but you wouldn't let me speak… I am so sorry for how I disrespected you, I was foolish for what I done. I came to my senses, and I left Jett the reason I am here today is to let him know…" Trivia said as her voice began cracking but she refused to shed a tear. "I am pregnant, but I don't want nothing from you Jett or do I want you around me and my baby," Trivia cried.

"Trivia how could you say that and do that to me?" Jett asked with compassion in his eyes.

"Hey what we did was wrong, and you know it was. I hurt someone very dear to me and then you turned around and hurt me. I never want to see you again," Trivia cried.

"Trivia, I'm sorry I was angry. You know how I feel about you," Jett pleaded.

"Goodbye Jett," Trivia said, walking out the door and just as she reached the door, she looked over her shoulders. "I am truly sorry for hurting you Mick I hope one day you find it in your heart to forgive me."

"Trivia! Trivia! Baby wait!" he yelled after her. But Jett was too late Trivia was gone and refused to turn back.

"What do you want?" he asked turning his attention to Mickie.

"First things first I ain't your punching bag anymore and you will not talk to me any kind of way anymore. I am happy and I've moved on with my life. I just want closure and an explanation why you did the things you did to me?" Mickie asked. "I was a good woman to you Jett Beverley."

"A good woman my butt you never listened to anything I said, you never kept my house clean, you got to the point you didn't wanna cook. How do you call that good?" Jett hissed at her.

"I did all those things, but you always wanted something to complain about it was like you were so miserable with me that you couldn't see the good in me," Mickie sneered.

"Do what? I did your sorry behind a favor by giving you the time a day no other man is going to put up with your bull crap and lazy butt," Jett snapped.

"That is where you are wrong Jett, I have a man that really cares about me standing outside but like a dang fool I'm in here trying to get closure from a narcissistic, manipulative, gaslighting individual your day is coming," Mickie snapped.

"Whatever… are you done," Jett laughed in her face.

"Go to hell, Jett," Mickie spat.

"I'm there now," he said.

Mickie stood and dashed out the room leaving Jett sitting there still laughing.

This was not the way she expected things to go when she went to visit Jett Beverley but like her mother used to always tell her, 'Everything happens for a reason."

The clicking of Mickie's foot and boot against the hard tile floor was all that could be heard as she made her way down the hallway out the view of the visitation area. Mickie wanted to be as far away from that room and Jett Beverley as she could.

How could I have been so naive to think Jett would take some responsibilities for his actions? Mickie asked herself.

It was no secret Mickie had expected her visit with Jett to go a lot differently.

"Why can't he take ownership for his wrongdoing? Why can't he admit he mistreated me?" She kept asking herself.

Forgive him for his wrong doings and move on my child. Mickie heard her mother's voice say to her just as clearly as if she was standing there with her at that very moment.

"Even not here Mama you are still guiding me. I love you and miss you so much," Mickie said. Mickie walked into the lobby and there was Kendal sitting patiently waiting on her. A smile became plastered across her face.

Why should I be worrying about Jett when God has sent a one-of-a-kind man just for me? Mickie said to herself. Mickie walked up to a Kendal and threw her arms around his neck.

"Thank you for being so patient and kind. I choose you and I choose us from now on," Mickie replied.

"I am so happy to hear you say that" Kendal said. "Are you ready to go grab a bite to eat and celebrate?" Kendal asked smiling down at Mickie.

"Celebrate what?" Mickie asked with a puzzled expression.

"Celebrate you finally coming to your senses and choosing us," Kendal laughed.

Mickie hit him in the arm. "Very funny Kendal."

Kendal pulled Mickie close to him and gazed into her eyes. "I love you Mickie with all of my heart, and I promise to always cherish and protect you."

"I know," Mickie said.
Mickie glanced back to the doors she just came out of.
Goodbye fear, heartache, and heartbreak.

~FORTY-SIX~

Frantically Laturi ran around her parents living room trying to adjust her bridal gown before her best friends came and waltz her off to the church. She looked so beautiful in her long white gown hugging her curvy body with sheer perfection and to top it off her long black hair was in a French braid all the way down her back with a tiara covering her head. Laturi was ready to catch anyone's attention.

"Look at my baby," her mother, Nadia gasped walking into the living room.

"How do I look Mama?" Laturi asked.

"Baby girl, you look amazing! You are the most beautiful bride I have ever seen," Nadia gushed.

"Thank you, Mama," Laturi pulled her mother into a hug.

"You seem a bit nervous," Nadia said.

"I am to be honest," Laturi said.

"Why are you nervous?" Nadia asked.

"I'm about to be a wife and I don't know how a wife be especially not good one. Mama I'm on edge I don't what kind of a wife I'm going to be," Laturi answered.

"Tour-Rie, you are going to be an amazing wife to Bron. Always pray and keep Christ first everything else will fall into place.

A gigantic smile came across Laturi's face.

"What are you smiling so big about?" Nadia asked.

"I never thought the day would come when I heard my mother talk about Jesus Christ and not have a bottle or glass in her hand," Laturi said.

"I awe it all to you, your prayers, and your faith in Jesus," Nadia said. "Now let's finish getting you dressed for your big day."

"Yes ma'am." Laturi took both her mother's hands into hers. "I love you so much Mama."

"I love you more."

Sha'Bron could feel the butterflies floating around in his stomach, his heartbeat was almost deafening to him.

"Hey son, you look a bit nervous," Stephon said.

"I am... I don't know anything about being a husband," Sha'Bron said.

"Son, listen to me being a husband and father doesn't come with a right or wrong, good, or bad manual but to trust and believe in God is going to be your key. There have been so many times I didn't know what to do or which way to turn but I prayed, and God brought me through. I promise you Bron he's going to do the same for you if you just trust him," Stephon replied.

"I know Dad, but I'm still having my doubts," Bron added.

"God has not given you the spirit of fear but of a sound body and mind," Stephon said.

"Dad, can you pray for me before the ceremony?" Bron asked with the sincerest look on his face.

Stephon walked behind his son and placed his hand on his shoulder. "Father God Lord Jesus I first wanna tell you thank you for bringing me and my son this far and allowing us to wake up this morning. God, I come to you asking you to give him the tools he needs to be a great husband to his soon to be wife. God bless their union in a way that only you can. In Jesus name amen."

"Thank you, Dad. I feel better already," Bron said.

"You are more than welcome son always keep God first and everything will fall into place," Stephon said.

The sound the processional music playing softly let Sha'Bron and Stephon know it was time.

"Well Dad, it's time for me to go say I do to the love of my life," Sha'Bron said.

"Most definitely, I am so excited and proud of you," Stephon said.

Sha'Bron nodded his head and gave his father a huge hug before taking a quick glance at his tie and tuxedo. When he realized he looked great. Sha'Bron walked towards the church entrance.

Sha'Bron felt like his heart was going to skip a beat when he gazed upon his future wife. Laturi looked stunning in her long white off the shoulder, trumpet gown hugging the natural curves of her small petite body. And when he looked into her eyes it felt as though her heart and soul were smiling at him.

I love you so much Laturi. Sha'Bron thought to himself.
Sha'Bron made a vow right then and there that he would always love her and protect her like he remembered his father always did for his mother.

~FORTY-SEVEN~

Shanti sat at the table beside Stephon holding his hand watching Sha'Bron and Laturi do their first dance together.

"I can't believe my biggest baby is married," Shanti gushed.

"Me either. It seems like yesterday we were just two college kids afraid as heck to tell our parents we had a baby on the way," Stephon reminisced.

"I remember that like it was yesterday. I knew my Daddy was going to kill you and blame you," Shanti said glancing into Stephon's eyes.

"And that he did, I blame you boy, you took advantage of my baby girl knowing she was innocent and naïve you are going to pay for this," Stephon quoted.

"Yes, at first you and Daddy didn't see eye to eye."

"Baby the only person in your family that cared for me was Me-Ma," Stephon replied.

"Me-Ma was the best she didn't take no sides she was for what was right," Shanti added.

"Most definitely. I am grateful for our life we made together and the amazing children we raised and raising together," Stephon said. Stephon leaned over and placed a kiss on Shanti's cheek.

"I love you Stephon Terrell Darwin," she purred kissing Stephon on the neck.

"I love you more Shanti Charlesia Darwin."

Sha'Bron pulled Laturi into a hug and gave her a passionate kiss on her lips. The loud chants and claps filled the room as the newlyweds continued their kiss. After a few moments they broke free from one another. Laturi hurried over to her parents' table while Sha'Bron hurried over his parents' table. "Mama, will you dance with me?" He asked Shanti with a huge smile plastered over his face.

Blushing and smiling Shanti replied. "Of course, baby."

Taking his mother by the hand and helping her from her seat. He locked his arm through his mother's arm and lead her to the dance floor. Shanti and Sha'Bron glanced over their shoulders and seen Laturi and her father.

"Because You Love Me" by Celine Dion began playing through the speakers.

"I wanna dedicate this song to the best mother in the world," Sha'Bron whispered.

"Thank you, baby," Shanti whispered trying to fight back tears.

"I love you, Mama."

"I love you more baby. I am so proud of the Godly man you have become," Shanti whispered in Sha'Bron ear.

"Thank you, Mama. I'm only this way because of how you and Dad raised me," he answered back.

Shanti could no longer hold back her tears; the tears began to flow down her cheeks like raindrops to say she was a proud mother at that moment was an understatement of how much joy she really felt.

The road had not been easy for her, but it was well worth it.

"Hey Dad, can we step outside and talk for a minute?" Sha'Bron walked over and whispered in Stephon's ear.

"Sure," Stephon said standing from his seat.

"What's wrong Babe?" Shanti asked.

"Nothing Baby I'm about to step outside with Sha'Bron really quick,"

The humid night air was a relief from the crowded ballroom floor.

Sha'Bron and his father took in a breath of fresh air. After a couple of moments of standing looking up at the stars Stephon was the first to speak.

"What's on your mind son?" Stephon asked.

"Well Dad, you know you and Mama's anniversary is only days away. Tour-Rie and I had planned to go on a weeklong cruise to The Virgin Islands for our honeymoon, but we decided to go to France instead. I would like you and Mama to go on the cruise instead along with all of your closest friends. It will be my anniversary gift to you,"

Sha'Bron announced.

"Oh…wow… son! I don't know what to say?" Stephon said.

"Say yes you will take the tickets and give Mama the time of her life," Sha'Bron said.

"Of course, thank you so much Bron," Stephon replied. Stephon grabbed his eldest son by his neck and pulled him into a hug. "You are the best son a father could ask for."

"Thanks Dad, same atcha," Sha'Bron replied.

Stephon had turned around heading for the door when Sha'Bron called after him.

"Dad don't tell Mama where you got the tickets. Make her think it was all your idea," Sha'Bron instructed his father.

~FORTY-EIGHT~

It was a quarter past six when Shanti finally finished her paperwork for the day and still trying to catch up from being on personal leave was very hectic on her.

Something in the back of her mind was telling her something significant was happening today but she was honestly too drained to even think about all it all was on her mind was getting home and resting from her long work week.

As she reached in her desk drawer to retrieve her purse and cell phone, her phone began playing. "Why I Love You So Much."

"Hey Baby," she purred.

"Hey yourself beautiful lady," her husband Stephon replied, "What are you up to?"

Pushing the desk drawer closed, and standing up, she replied, "Nothing much getting ready to leave the office and come home to you."

"Oh yeah? Haven't you forgotten something?" He quizzed.

"No, not that I know of," she answered through squinted eyes, something she always did when thinking. Then, she ran her hand through her long relaxed black hair, before walking out her office and locking the door.

"Okay, that really hurts my feelings. You don't remember the day you became Mrs. Darwin," he announced.

"Oh shoot, it's today?" Shanti shrieked.

"Yes, ma'am it is. Happy twentieth anniversary, Baby."

"Thank you, Babe, same to you. Goodness, I can't believe I

completely forgot. I'm so sorry. Between me getting back on track here at work, and the kids it totally slipped my mind," she pleaded.

"Hey Beautiful, it's okay. I was waiting all day for you to call, and when you never did, I knew you must have forgotten. It's all good though, I do have something special planned for you tonight," he teased.

"Really? What?" Shanti asked, not at all trying to hide her excitement.

"Well, Mrs. Darwin, the first thing I got you is a hair, nails, and spa appointment at Talia's salon. And later on, tonight I have a few special reservations planned."

"Oh, my goodness! Baby you are the best what did I ever do to deserve you!" Shanti squealed.

"You're not the lucky one, I am."

"Awe, you are so sweet. I love you so much!" Shanti gushed.

"I love you more, Beautiful. Now hurry up so you don't miss your appointment," Stephon said before ending the call.

Shanti smiled as she made her way through the parking garage to her vehicle. Once she was close enough, she hit the remote to unlock her 2022 midnight blue BMW convertible. She threw her purse into the passenger seat before pressing the ignition button and driving off. When she pulled into the parking lot of Talia's Hair and nail Salon and placed the gear in park, she noticed the vehicles of four of her best friends and immediately knew they'd been waiting for her to get there. "That Stephon," she said aloud through a huge smile, and jumped out her car to rush inside.

"About time you got here," Casmira huffed jokingly as soon Shanti walked inside.

"Well hello to you too, Heifah," Shanti laughed.

"See, today is your special day so Imma let you have that one," Casmira sarcastically replied.

"Why thank you," Shanti laughed again.

"Happy twenty-year anniversary!" Audria, Talia, and Yasmine bellowed in unison running over to her and hugging her.

"Aww, thank you, guys," Shanti sang, wiping away imaginary tears.

"Girl, twenty years is a long time to be with the same man," Audria admitted without hesitation.

Audria was five feet and five inches tall, with a butterscotch skin complexion, thin lips that were glossy from her lip gloss, a Nubian nose, light brown close-set eyes, and shoulder length black hair.

"Yeah, it is, but you know what? I love him just as much, if not more, than I did when we first fell in love," Shanti confessed, with undeniable love and adoration in her eyes.

"Oh honey, I know you do," Casmira chimed in. "It seems like yesterday we were in junior high, and you had the hugest crush on him," she recalled.

"Shanti had it so bad for Sty it was almost pathetic," Yasmine laughed. Yasmine was five feet and two inches tall, with a chestnut skin complexion, a heavy lower lip that stayed glossy from her lip gloss, a button nose, almond shaped mahogany brown eyes and shoulder length silky black hair hanging down her back parted down the middle.

Remember that time she wrote him a letter, sprayed some of her perfume on it, and put it in his locker?"

"Hey, what can I say?" Shanti shrugged, "That letter got me a date with him, and we've been going strong ever since. Wait..." Shanti said, scanning the salon, "Where in the world is Rasheia?"

"Well, she told me she wasn't going to be able to make it," Casmira answered.

"And why not?" Shanti huffed.

Casmira folded her arms and shrugged, "She sounded pissed. Said Rashad came home super late last night, and they've been at each other's throats all day."

"Oh Lord," Shanti rolled her eyes.

"Right!" Talia said, shaking her head, "But anyway, girl, Sty called me last night right before closing and made an appointment for you. He offered to pay, but I told him this would be my anniversary gift to you," Talia smiled as she reached out and grabbed Shanti into a hug. Talia was a little hood, but she was highly educated. She had a warm honey skin complexion; downward lips and her S-shaped eyebrows complimented her piercing green almond shaped eyes.

"Omg! Thank you, Talia."

Shanti took a seat down in the chair across from Audria, and Casmira sat down in the chair across from Talia's coworker Mia.

"So, what's been up with you all?" Shanti asked, making herself comfortable in the soft cushioned salon chair.

"Hmm, where do I even begin? Well for starters, since Gabe started having more clientele, he's never home; and when he is, he doesn't pay me any mind just the boys," Audria complained.

"Audria you should be glad his business is booming, that means more money for y'all," Shanti reminded her.

"I know Shanti, but I wanna be able to spend time with him. When he is home, he is on the computer, asleep or doing stuff with the boys. I be wanting at least some of his attention," Audria groaned.

"Audria. Gabe built that trucking company from the ground up. Do you remember how many nights he stayed awake and cried because he wanted to be successful," Shanti recounted.

"How do you know about that?" Audria asked.

"I know because he called Stephon asking him questions and talking over his fears of failure. The main person he never wanted to fail was you," Shanti confessed to Audria.

At that moment all the talking and laughing came to a halt. Audria sat back in her chair and grabbed her face, "I didn't know that" she muttered more to herself than anyone else.

"I'm sorry if I upset you Audria," Shanti said.

"No, I needed to hear that. Y'all excuse me I need to make a phone call," Audria said, standing up and walking outside.

"So, Cassie, how's life treating you?" Shanti asked.

"I'm ready for God to send my husband so I'll have help. I'm tired of everything falling back on me," Casmira said.

"In due time God is going to send you the perfect man and he's going to love you the way you deserve to be loved," Shanti assured her.

"I know Shani but I'm so tired of being lonely and playing the role of superwoman," Casmira whined.

"I would rather be alone any day than settle for anything and as a beautiful black queen you are superwoman with or without a man's help.," Shanti said.

"I know and believe me I'm no longer settling. I'm waiting for God to send my Boaz," Casmira said.

"Like Pastor Laughlin said last week ladies wait for your Boaz stop settling for his cousins such as broke Az, lying AZ, cheating Az, and so many others," Talia chimed in.

"I know that's right, cause y'all know I've had my experience with all of them and some," Casmira said.

Casmira, Shanti, and Talia were busy in a conversation, but Yasmine was sitting in the corner to herself staring off into space. Casmira was the first to notice her.

"Yasmine what's wrong honey?"

Yasmine looked up briefly, "Nothing just got a lot on my mind."

"Like what? What's wrong?" Talia asked.

"It's nothing you guys, I'm good, really" Yasmine reassured them.

"Yasmine we've all been friends for years. You don't gotta hide anything from us," Casmira stated.

"I know, I know Cassie," Yasmine said barely above a whisper.

A few minutes later Stephon strolled into the salon.

"Hey ladies," he said.

"Wow that's a good looking brutha right there," Talia joked.

"Hey Talia. How are you, Sis?" Stephon said walking over to give her a hug.

"I'm good, happy anniversary to you!" Talia stated.

"Thank ya, thank ya," Stephon replied.

Shanti stood up from her seat and sashayed over to Stephon embracing him.

"You look all dolled up, are you ready for tonight?" he asked.

"What exactly is happening tonight, Mr. Darwin?" Shanti quizzed.

Stephon leaned in as close to her ear as possible and whispered, "It's a surprise," before planting a soft kiss on her ear. "Ladies," he said, as he looked in the direction of Shanti's friends, "I'll see y'all this evening," he replied and walked towards the door. As he opened it and began walking out, he yelled over his shoulder, "And Cassie keep yo mouth shut."

Everyone laughed.

"Whatever Sty! You act like I can't hold water," Casmira yelled back.

"Um you can't," Stephon said, as he threw up his hand in a wave and walked to his car.

Shanti sat back in her chair, folded her arms, and crossed her legs, "Okay chick, go ahead and spill the tea."

"No ma'am," Casmira shook her head quickly, "I made a promise to Sty that I gotta keep this time," she chuckled, "but girl I will say this is going to be an anniversary to remember."

Shanti looked out the window and watched Stephon pull off with a smile plastered on her face. That man still gave her butterflies.

~FORTY-NINE~

Shanti's mouth dropped the moment the black matte classic Cadillac limousine pulled into the driveway. Stephon had really outdone himself this time. Obviously, he was deeply committed to making their twentieth anniversary the best one yet. Frantically, Shanti ran down the hall to the bathroom to check herself for the last time. She was a beautiful woman inside and out. Standing at five foot seven inches tall, she had a warm honey-brown complexion, flawless skin, and an hourglass shape. The royal blue A-line halter knee length dress hugged her curves with sheer perfection. If that wasn't enough, her long black hair hung down her back in curls making her ready to demand attention in any room. Turning away from the floor length mirror, Shanti glanced over her shoulder to give herself one final inspection and after smiling at her reflection, she headed outside where her limousine awaited.

"Good afternoon Mrs. Darwin," the polite young gentleman greeted, giving her a quick bow.

"Good afternoon to you too, Sir," Shanti replied.

The young man held Shanti's hand as she took her seat inside. Waiting for her was a bottle of champagne being chilled in ice, a dozen white and pink roses just like on their prom night, and a card on perfect display inside the roses. Shanti felt like a giddy teenager. She couldn't contain her excitement as she grabbed the card and ripped it open.

Happy anniversary to the most beautiful, amazing woman on the face of the earth. Thank you for twenty awesome years of being my wife and best friend. I know I am not the perfect husband, but I strive to be, daily. I hope that you are happy with everything I did for you tonight. You deserve this, and so much more. Shoot, to be honest, If I could buy you the world in a heartbeat, I would; and that still wouldn't be enough. I love you Shanti Charlesia Darwin, with all my heart and soul. Thank you again for twenty amazing years of marriage.

A tear fell from her eyes as she read the note Stephon had written her. Things had not been a fairytale between them, but they made the best of it. She thought about after they married fresh out of college with a newborn baby. They were young and had no clue. Her lifelong dream had been to become a doctor, like her mother, but due to having her son during her sophomore year of college she put her dreams on hold. Stephon wanted to make sure Shanti achieved her dream. He dropped out of college to try and make it easier for her to graduate. He would always say, "Baby you are going to finish school and you're going to get your medical degree."

As much as she wanted to believe him, there was always a part of her that said it was just a dream. She would never forget the day he came in from work and yelled for her to come into the living room. She'd grabbed their son Sha'Bron and walked into the living room. Before she could say anything, he looked down at her with a sparkle in his eyes she had never seen before.

"Baby," Stephon smiled as he placed the baby inside his crib and took Shanti by both of her hands as they both eased down on the sofa, "All I wanna hear is a yes or no answer, okay."

She nodded her head in agreement.

"Do you still wanna finish school?"

"Yes, Babe. More than anything," she blurted out.

"Well in August you start your new semester!" Stephon yelled.

"You're kidding me, right?" Shanti asked, feeling the tears forming in her eyes.

"Not at all. Make your dreams come true, girl. Don't worry about a thing. I got you."

That was the type of man she had married; a man who would do anything to make her happy.

"Mrs. Darwin, we're here," the young gentleman replied, interrupting her thoughts.

She waited as he opened the driver's door, walked around to the back passenger side door, and opened it for Shanti. The moment she stepped out of the vehicle, her eyes landed on Stephon, standing there decked out in a black Giorgio Armani suit.

"My, my, my, Mrs. Darwin, you are one fine woman," Stephon admired, grabbing her hand, and kissing it. He chuckled when he lifted his eyes and noticed Shanti blushing. It made him feel good knowing he still had that effect on her. "So, how'd you like your ride?" He asked, hooking her arm in his.

Shanti smiled, "It was a nice fit for a queen."

"Well, you are definitely a queen, beautiful," Stephon said as the host led them through the crowded restaurant, and then through another door to the back of the establishment –the VIP section. There was a small couple's table centered between five other round tables three to the left and two on the right. The couple's table had a royal blue tablecloth and a silver centerpiece that had pink flowers inside a vase. The flowers were covered with rhinestones, and there was a small card with their names written on it. The other tables had pink plastic tablecloths with royal blue roses inside. The arrangement and ambiance actually made Shanti gasp.

"I wanted everything to be perfect for tonight?" Stephon said as he dismissed the host and held out the seat for Shanti. He waited as she took her seat and then took a couple of steps to the other side of the table to join her.

Shanti leaned forward, "So what's all going on tonight?"

"You will see in due time," he replied.

A few minutes later Talia, and her husband Jacob, walked inside the room.

"This is nice Sty you out did yourself this time bro," Talia said, giving Shanti and Stephon a big hug. Jacob did the same before sitting at the table across from them.

A few minutes later all their closest friends were sitting around them at different tables. Shanti was happy to see that Rasheia and Rashad were able to make it as well.

Shortly after, a young bubbly waitress appeared, took their drink orders, cracked a few jokes, and left a menu on each table before leaving them to the laughter she'd caused.

After they all calmed down, Stephon stood up and addressed them, "I would first like to say thank you guys for coming out to celebrate Shanti and me on our anniversary. I know a couple of you know already, but others do not. The guys and I got together and chimed in to pay for a seven-day couple's cruise. I also have something special planned for Mrs.," Stephon winked at Shanti.

"I can't wait to see the surprise," Casmira teased, pointing at Shanti playfully.

Shanti giggled.

Stephon continued, "I found this bible scripture I wanna read to my lovely wife. First Shanti, you helped me find myself and introduced me to Christ, and I love you for that. I was on my way to spending a lifetime in jail, or committing crime, but you did something nobody else ever did, Baby —you believed in me. This scripture comes to mind when I think of you. *A wife of noble character who can find. She is worth far more than rubies. Her husband has full confidence in her and lacks nothing of value. She brings him good, not harm, all the days of her life.* This is you and so much more. Again, I say Happy Anniversary to my wife, my best friend, and my good thang," Stephon said, helping Shanti to her feet and pulling her in for a kiss.

She broke free briefly to mouth the words, "I love you too, Stephon."

And they continued their passionate kiss while listening to the echoes of their best friends chanting and cheering in the background.

~EPILOGUE~

One Year Later.

Mickie took one final glance at herself in the mirror.

"I can't believe today is my wedding day?" Mickie said to herself. Mickie had been through a lot in the last past couple of years and even months that her getting married to a man that loves her like Kendal Gardener was only a sweet fantasy.

"Knock! Knock!" Lauryn and Shanti squealed in unison marching into the room. Lauryn looked beautiful in her floor length Lilac Matron of Honor gown.

"Hey, you too," Mickie shrieked with excitement.

"Auntie, you look amazing you are one of the prettiest brides I've seen," Shanti gushed.

"Thank you, baby girl," Mickie said pulling her niece into a hug.

"I am so proud of you and happy for you," Lauryn said. "You are one beautiful bride."

"Well thank you Laurie and thank you for never giving up on me," Mickie said.

"I'm your older sister I would never give up on you," Lauryn said.

"It's like Mama used to always say you two are all you got in this world," Mickie said.

Lauryn reached out and squeezed Mickie's hands. "You are right!"

"C'mon Mama and Auntie let's not turn a happy occasion into a sad one Me-Ma would be very proud of all of our accomplishments," Shanti chimed in.

The three ladies locked arms and hugged one another.

"I miss her so much," Mickie said.

"I do too," Lauryn said.

"She is smiling down on us," Shanti said.

"I know but I do wanna say this… I understand what Mama was talking about on her death bed when she said those scriptures to me. I have learned to put God first and everything else has fell into place," Mickie said.

There was a knock at the door.

"That better not be Kendal trying to see you before the ceremony," Lauryn hissed walking towards the door. Lauryn swung open the door and her husband Charles was standing there. "Hey babe, let Mickie know they are ready for her to make her grand entrance," Charles said.

Shanti hurried and walked into the hallway and hooked arms with Stephon.

Sha'Bron hooked arms with Harmony and Xavion hooked arms with Azure.

"You are going to make a wonderful wife Mickie," Charles whispered in Mickie's ear as he locked arms with her.

Johnny Gill's "You For Me" began to play from the speakers. All the onlookers kept their eyes on Mickie as she marched down the aisle, but her attention was focused on Kendal. Kendal looked amazing in his all-white pant suit and lilac tie.

"I love you with all my heart," Kendal mouthed to Mickie.

"I love you too," Mickie mouthed back. And for the first time in both of their lives they knew the love they shared in their hearts for the other person was reciprocated.

Mickie and Charles made their way down the aisle. Mickie looked up at Kendal with love and admiration in her eyes. "I am so happy for you," Charles whispered in Mickie's ear before taking his seat on the front row.

"The couple decided to write their own vows. Ms. Pearson and Mr. Gardener speak from your hearts," Minister Ryan announced.

Mickie reached out both of her small brown hands and placed them into Kendal's hands. A big bright smile was plastered across her face as tears began to flow down like rain.

"Kendal Gardener, I never thought in a million years that I would be able to take vows before God for a man that loves me unconditionally and holds my heart in his hands. My life has been a fast rollercoaster ride, but the day God allowed you to enter into my life and into my heart. I knew he must have really loved me to send such a gentle, loving soul to care for me. I vow to always love you, protect you and stand by your side as long as we both shall live," Mickie vowed, as tears flowed down her cheeks.

"Mickie, in a world of pain and suffering I never would have imagined finding such an angel on heart. You are truly a blessing from heaven and a gift from God himself. I promise to never hurt you or disrespect you in any type of way. I promise to always love you and protect you as long as we both shall live," Kendal vowed.

"After that there is nothing more to say. I now pronounce you Mr. And Mrs. Kendal Gardener," Minister Ryan annunciated.

Kendal pulled Mickie into a romantic hug and kissed her lips passionately sealing their love and commitment to one another.

The church erupted into chants and applause as they continued their passionate kiss.

~ WORD FROM THE AUTHOR ~

Dear Reader,

   I would first like to say thank you for choosing my book. I hope that you all fell in love with the characters just as I did when I created them.

   I begin writing this novel many years ago and never thought once to publish it until I let a couple people read my notes and each one of them told me I needed to do something with my talent.

   Each one of my characters had their own thoughts and personalities; some you liked and some not so much. Just like everyday people they went through some very trying times in their lives and by the grace of God they overcome.

   This book also dealt with death of a loved one, depression, betrayal, abuse, and heartbreak things that many of us face but are afraid to talk about.

   I would love to hear feedback from my readers. Feel free to email me at authorfrancinerachelle89@gmail.com or on Facebook at Author Ra'Chelle Dixon. I will be waiting to hear back from you. God bless each one of you.

   -FR.

~ ACKNOWLEDGEMENTS ~

First and foremost, I would like to thank **Jesus** for giving me the talent and passion for writing. I stray away many times, but I have always found my way back and I owe it all to you. I want to say thank you for all the trials and tribulations that you have allowed me to face to help me bring my story together even more so that you can get all the glory. I promise to use my talent only for your glory!

My Daddy Willie, thank you for being the best father in the world. You taught me what kind of man to look for in a husband. I love you and miss you so much continue to rest in God's loving arms.

Andreya, "Hanna/Dreya" I love you cuz. Thank you for believing in me and encouraging me to chase my dreams. You are the best!

Rie and Vic, thank you for being the best parents in the world, for believing in me, and encouraging me to set goals and achieve them no matter what. Those words "there is no limit to your success" stay with me and motivate me to strive even harder. I love you both and again thank you!

Aunt Mary, Wayne, Red and China, thank you for your love and your support and believing in me I love y'all.

My TLC (The Lighthouse Church) Family, thank you so much for accepting me into your family thank you all for your love and support. You all are one of a kind. I could not have chosen a better church family!

Andrea and La'Grace, thank you for your love and support throughout the years, and being the older sisters I needed in my life. Thank you for praying for me constantly. I love you both!

Dylan, Yada, and Yisey, I love the three of you like you are my own. I will forever be in your corner and have y'all's back. I love you guys more than life.

Donnie McClurkin and Kirk Franklin, you two will never know the impact you had on my life, your music ministered to my soul in a way you can never imagine. When I lost my mom at twelve your music helped me through just like many other challenging times in my life. You two are truly anointed by God. I wish to one day meet you both and tell you in person how you helped me throughout my life.

Tamika, you have been my best friend since we were kids, you have always been my go-to person. I love you!

Jessica, thank you for coming into my life and being a real friend. You are an amazing and beautiful person inside and out. I am forever grateful to have you as my best friend and sister. I love you, Sis!

Author A.W. Myrie, thank you so much for helping me and beginning this writing journey with me. I learned so much from you and your writing style. I am forever grateful for the opportunity to get to know you and work with you. God Bless!

My Best Friend, thank you for your support, encouraging words, and being the best co-writer ever you helped me through so many times of writer's block. You never allowed me to give up on myself or my dream. I appreciate you!

Author Tosha Writes, my newfound writing friend thank you so much for your support and helping me to get my writing career started.

Keith Kareem Williams, thank you for helping my dreams of becoming a published author come true! You are the best thank you for all of your hard work and dedication to my book. I can't wait to work with you again soon!

To everyone that believed in me that I did not call by name, thank you so much for your support!

I love you all. -FR

ABOUT THE AUTHOR

Francine Ra'Chelle, is a new writer and Alabama native. Born and raised in a small southern town named Elba, in her free time she enjoys spending time with family and friends, reading books, writing and chasing after her beloved fur babies Riley and Molly.

Made in the USA
Columbia, SC
04 November 2024

151f1e38-4308-4cd0-bbfe-89bda79a60e2R02